Advance Praise for *Journey*

"Author Stephen Foreman's electrifying *Journey* takes us on a wild, emotional ride with three mesmerizing, unforgettable characters in the Old West of the 1830s. Stephen's prowess as both an author and screenwriter are in full display as we actually see and feel every moment of the adventure. Unlike most westerns, the title character of *Journey* is a courageous, irrepressible young woman whose indomitable spirit comes alive like a flaming arrow on each page. Set against the backdrop of social challenges such as slavery and intolerance that still resonate today, *Journey* is a spellbinding page turner that reminds us of how captivating a great story and characters can be in the hands of a master story teller. What a great book—can't wait to the see the movie."
—Stephen Simon, producer of the films *Somewhere in Time, What Dreams May Come,* and *All The Right Moves*

"Raw, gritty, unflinching, yet still somehow tender. A gripping tale about freedom, identity, heritage. A Western unlike any you've read before."—Casey Scieszka, author of *To Timbuktu: Nine Countries, Two People, One True Story*

"This stirring tale thrusts the reader into the 1830s of the West. It's an eye-opening depiction of the savagery and magnificence of the period. It redefines and reanimates our conventional notions of the Western saga. The characters are vividly drawn. The writing style is almost painterly. It's visual and seems like a firsthand account of actual events. Mr. Foreman transports us to a world that is recognizable and at the same time fresh and enthralling."—Tony Shalhoub, Emmy- and Golden Globe-winning actor

"Although identified as "a western" in its subtitle, this briskly paced novel by Stephen Foreman bursts the traditional bounds of the genre. Set in a harsh Southwest still beyond the edge of the law, its vividly constructed characters take the reader on a wild horseback ride through rugged country, villainy, nature's ferocity, and the evil of slavery on the frontier. Few will forget the journey."—E. Donnall Thomas Jr., author of *How Sportsmen Saved the World* and *Montana Streams, Peaks and Prairies*

"*Journey*, set in the American West before the Civil War, tells the vivid story of three people who struggle to make lives in a still raw and brutal country: Journey is an astonishingly capable sixteen year old whose background is a mystery and who seems to have been all but born on horseback; Reuben Moon, part Mexican and part Apache, a tracker and a hunter who carries within him the gifts of the mountains and the woods and may also be Journey's father; and Esau Burdock, a wealthy slave trader who was born poor and didn't forget it. The land was rich with wild food and wilder animals, including a mountain lion as vivid as Journey herself. The book's considerable power comes from Foreman's deep understanding of an America two hundred years ago, run on a slave economy. This is a first rate American novel with haunting characters in the spirit of Larry McMurtry."—David Freeman, screenwriter

"A book of historical importance, as *Journey* is, usually delivers the stuff that satisfies readers. But Stephen Foreman's achievement with Journey is to combine historically accurate facts with riveting fiction, creating a book of tremendous importance. Read, enjoy, and reflect on Journey's journey and her emancipation. I loved this book!"—Joseph B. Healy, editor of *When Bears Attack*

"Reading this book I was swept into a compelling narrative as raw and bold as the old Southwest. We forget how very different we are, yet how connected we can be by events bigger than ourselves. Foreman's story starts with the meteor shower that stunned and shocked everyone whose eyes were opened to the sky on a November night in 1833. And we cannot help but ride along with the girl who stares at the sky from the back of her paint pony. It was a seminal moment in the lives of all who witnessed the Leonid meteor shower of November 18, 1833. All over the continent eyes were turned to the heavens in wide wonder and fear. This story opens with Journey sitting on a paint pony beneath an angry sky. She wonders what it is going to mean and we do too, swept along with her into Foreman's epic of incest, injustice and instinct."—Gary Lewis, host of *Frontier Unlimited*, author of *John Nosler Going Ballistic*

"The boundaries of color and caste have been breached, tweaked, and traversed in these United States of America even before its formal inception as a nation. And Stephen Foreman fuses compassion, astuteness, and vigorous prose to bring these elements to an antebellum western whose heroic values are at once familiar and fresh. You can almost feel the prairie breezes and night chills on your skin along with *Journey*'s heroine, who fears nothing in her past or present."—Gene Seymour

"After reading *Journey*, no one will think the same way about the Old West or slavery. This beautifully told tale of love, hate, and courage, with its superb descriptions of western landscape, complex and nuanced characters, vengeance and forgiveness, is a fine work of art."—Luke Salisbury, author of *Hollywood and & Sunset*, *The Cleveland Indian*, and *The Answer Is Baseball*

"Stephen H. Foreman takes the reader on a wild ride in Journey, a stage coach of a novel with its bumps, twists and turns that spans from the then New Mexico Territory to New Orleans and London with its Dickensian overtones. With an Apache Indian maiden as the focal point, Foreman in this adventure novel gives the reader a plot twist that is worthy of Sophocles."—Dolan Hubbard, PhD, Chairperson, Department of English and Language Arts, Morgan State University

JOURNEY

JOURNEY:

A WESTERN

STEPHEN H. FOREMAN

Skyhorse Publishing

Skyhorse Publishing books may be purchased in bulk at special discounts for sales promotion, corporate gifts, fund-raising, or educational purposes. Special editions can also be created to specifications. For details, contact the Special Sales Department, Skyhorse Publishing, 307 West 36th Street, 11th Floor, New York, NY 10018 or info@skyhorsepublishing.com.

Skyhorse® and Skyhorse Publishing® are registered trademarks of Skyhorse Publishing, Inc.®, a Delaware corporation.

Visit our website at www.skyhorsepublishing.com.

10 9 8 7 6 5 4 3 2 1

Library of Congress Cataloging-in-Publication Data is available on file.

Cover design by Tom Lau
Cover photo credit Brian Peterson

Print ISBN: 978-1-5107-1704-6
Ebook ISBN: 978-1-5107-1705-3

Printed in the United States of America

To Sophie Shalhoub, my fearless and beloved goddaughter, whose rambunctious and indomitable spirit animates this story.

Contents

Book 1

Journey: When We First See Her

—◦◦◦—

November 18, 1833
The Sangre de Christo Mountains
New Mexico Territory

SOJOURNER, SIXTEEN YEARS TODAY, CALLED JOURNEY BY THOSE who know her, sat her paint pony bareback on the mountain top under the black November nighttime sky and held her breath as she watched dozens, and tens of dozens, of fire balls streak down from a deep and distant heaven. The sky heaved with an endless cascade of white-hot traces. She had seen shooting stars before: brief kindles of light gone before you blinked. One or two a night–four, maybe, if she stared real hard, and then she'd better be looking in the right place. But this was different. No matter where she looked she saw them: rocks flung from long ago before time. That's what the old people said. They said first life came to Earth this way.

Some of the rocks came with thunder, not a blustery outburst, but a furious crack like the sound an axe handle would make if you snapped it across your knee. No wind. No rain.

1

Only streaks of light and random shots. It was unusually warm for this time of year, and her deerskin leggings and over blouse were enough to keep the chill away. A leather band braided like a rein kept her hair out of her eyes, but the rest of it tumbled about her head and neck in an untamed fall of rowdy curls so blonde as to be nearly white. A feather from a wild turkey was shoved upside down into her headband and hung down over her left ear. Come autumn, when the pods of the bull thistle burst and send their seeds through the air, some always settled in the thicket of her hair. Sometimes a leaf or a piece of one was caught up in it, too. Or a twig. Once a tiny fragment of pale green eggshell. Once a piece of blue thread.

Journey knew caution, but she didn't know fear. She wore two amulets around her neck: One had been carved for her from a piece of oak struck by lightning; the other was carved from a green stone by ancient hands long passed, and so Journey felt watched over when she roamed the mountain night and day at will. The knife at her side, traded for at a rendezvous north on the Green River when she was old enough, had never been drawn to do much more than whittle traps and whistles and cages for little animals, though she'd skinned with it, too, and made arrows. Her father, for that's how she knew him, taught her how, and helped her make a bow. Her first hunting season he called in a wild turkey for her, though it was her shot that took the bird at the juncture of his neck and his chest. She was calm; her arrow went true. She took game from an early age and hardly missed.

She'd been there on the mountain as evening came on, when the owls began to call each other. Usually, when the sun was nearly down, one heard scurrying and rustling under the dry leaves; a stick might snap, a rock slip. Creatures moving. Warm air rising from the valley often brought with it the scent of winter pelts, but a late rainfall had scrubbed the sky clean.

Everything had stopped to look. The clouds moved on, and now only the blind could ignore the barrage above. Oh, to fly like that! To straddle one of those balls of fire! To *be* the heat and not get burnt; to ride it faster than a thousand horses; to hear its roar! She was lost in that swarm of fire. The edges of her soul had melted. Time didn't exist.

A sudden crack, louder and nearer than any she'd yet heard, made the horse kick and startled her so much that Journey nearly fell. One fireball had dropped below the moon and seemed on an arrow's flight toward where she watched. She couldn't look elsewhere, and wondered as the wind rushed over her head if a ghost were coming to take her. She felt the wind and the warm air as the fireball passed, but none of its fury as it was still above the trees. Yet on it came and nothing to stop it as every foot brought it closer to the earth until, for a few breathless bits of seconds, it disappeared into a canyon some ways over and finally exploded with a shock of light in the gravel bed of a dry creek. The impact sent sharp-edged pieces of stone flying in an expanding circle as if they were grapeshot. Journey heard them clatter on the rocks. A mule deer somewhere out there bleated in pain, but Journey was still alive and untouched, and not at all surprised by that.

The night sky continued to blaze away—it was as if the air were filled with burning arrows—but Journey could reckon the area of impact by the fixed and visible stars that were to-night what they were yesterday and would be tomorrow. What she also knew was that her eyes were not the only ones to mark its fall. Others would light torches and climb the mountain. They'd probably started already. Journey dismounted and led her horse across the face toward the canyon, picking her way like a creature that lived there. It wasn't far. She closed the distance quickly and found a gentle slope she could ride to the canyon floor. Once there it was too dark to see, so she ground hitched her horse, then sat down with her back against a rock and waited for the light. She'd got up a sweat crossing the mountain, and now the chill began to work its way through her buckskins. Journey had flint and tinder in a pouch worn around her waist. She could have made a fire, warmed herself. But, not wanting to give away her position, she simply wrapped her arms around her knees and waited. She shivered, yet sat there patiently, knowing dawn would come, and, when it did Journey opened her eyes and took stock of where she was.

The crater was nearly at her feet, big around as a buffalo wallow and deep as two men are tall. She'd seen one much bigger over west in the Tonto territory, but that happened before there was anyone to remember it. This one was still warm. A tendril of smoke rose from its center, and beyond, on the far lip of the crater just opposite her, sat a mountain lion as quiet and unblinking as she was. It was a big cat, heavily muscled, with a head like a boulder. When she got to her feet the lion was gone. To glimpse a creature like that, if only for an instant (and an instant is all there ever is), was a wonder Journey prized dearly.

She walked to the edge of the crater and peered into it. The earth was warm under her moccasins, and she could feel heat rising from the pit itself. Not so much as to burn, though. Suddenly, Journey wanted to be down there on the spot where the fireball hit. As close as possible. Protruding rocks would give her footholds. It wouldn't be very hard, and, in seconds she found herself on the floor of the crater.

As the morning light made its way down to where Journey stood, she examined the walls and explored them with her hands. They were no different than she had seen many times before, and she felt deflated. She had expected what? She didn't know exactly, but whatever change might have been she knew hadn't happened. Journey took her knife, pried loose a promising stone from the pit wall and turned it over, looking for evidence of an ancient tree or a beetle, but she tossed it aside impatiently when she found exactly nothing. She concentrated instead on where she stood.

The sunlight reached the floor of the crater and pooled around her feet, giving her elk hide moccasins an amber hue. Journey squatted and explored the floor. Except for the spot from where the smoke rose, the stones were warm but not unpleasant to touch. With the sun rising, the pool of light widened to take in the entire crater, so things stood out in clear relief. Stones. Stones. Stones. None unusual, except for the one from where the smoke rose. It was black, though none of the others were, and stuck in the ground so she couldn't pry it out. She kicked and kicked, and finally pried it loose. Journey tested it with her finger to see how hot it was. She had an ancient Mexican army canteen with her, and knowing how close she was to home she emptied the water from the canteen over the black rock. It sizzled, and she kicked it. The black rock split in two. One side, the blackest, continued to send out wisps of smoke. Journey turned the stone so she could study it, and saw that its face was embedded with a myriad of lucent crystals, each the size of a grain of sand. This was a treasure—one she would never have far from reach.

Journey hadn't eaten since yesterday afternoon, and her stomach was none too happy about it. A corn cake; goat's milk; jerky. That'd be good. She tested the wall for a foothold, found one, reached above her, and, with the stone in her left hand, Journey put her head down and began to climb. It wasn't a difficult climb at all, but as she neared the top she looked up and was startled to see the mountain lion sitting on the ledge above her head staring down at her. She stopped climbing but the animal made no move. It simply sat there and stared at her.

They locked eyes. Journey hollered and hollered again, but it wouldn't move. From somewhere below on the mountain she heard a man's voice holler out an answer. The cat heard it, too, turned its eyes away, and faded back into the rocks.

————⤳∞⤴————

Mescalero Apache Territory
New Mexico
May 18, 1829

WHEN JOURNEY WAS ABOUT TO COME OF AGE, HER godmother, an Apache woman whose nose had been cut off as punishment for adultery, took her outside the village boundaries to build a special dwelling with its entrance to the east, where she would live for a month while the women of the tribe taught her their ways. It would take that long to prepare for the final ceremony, although Journey had been building her endurance by running beyond exhaustion for years. She was not born of the tribe, but had been brought to them as a newborn. The woman who would become her godmother rarely left her dwelling out of shame. The child of her illicit union died soon after birth, but her breasts were still heavy with milk when the newborn came. She awoke one morning to find an eagle feather on a stone outside the entrance to her dwelling, and understood she had been chosen. Journey took to the woman's breasts like a cannibal, and though there was pain the woman was grateful, and rocked her and sang to her and kept her warm.

The first thing Journey learned in her dwelling was that First Woman, when she was old, walked toward the sun, met her young self, and became young again. She was covered with a mixture of corn meal and clay, then dusted with cattail pollen, and had to stay so for four days. She had to be fed by others, and was forbidden to scratch without using a special scratch stick. When she was not dancing she was running, running, running to the four winds. Four days. No sleep. She carried a feather stick that she would use again much later, when she was old. She endured having her hair pulled, for that meant longer life. She tossed babies high up in the air to the four directions, and healed the sick who came to her. At the end of four weeks, she spent the night praying and fasting. She wore nothing but a buffalo robe. When dawn approached, she removed the robe and dropped to her knees before the open entrance of her dwelling, spread them, leaned back with her arms behind her, and waited for the sun to rise– for its first ray to strike her womb. When the first bright drop of blood appeared, her ordeal was over.

———∞∞∞———

Reuben Moon
November 18, 1833
Mescalero Apache Territory

Tonight's storm, with its cannonade of cosmic fireballs, took Reuben Moon back to one similar, from sixteen years past, when he happened upon a creature that clung to him forever. That night, Wild Horse Canyon had funneled a fury of water down from Trapper Peak and sent it raging through the canyon like a battering ram. The night before had been so crisp and clean that the stars seemed near enough to grab. Then, when dawn came and the sky should have lightened, it darkened instead as if a blanket were dropped over the morning sun. Reuben rode with his back hunched to the storm and let the paint horse pick its way. It was a good mountain pony and had seen worse, as had its rider, but this storm featured a stabbing rain that chilled to the bones. Reuben could have searched out an overhang or hollow in the rocks where he might build a fire and wait out the storm, but he was certain the baby would die if he stopped. It was only a few hours old, a little girl no bigger than a puppy that Reuben cupped in his hand inside his buckskin shirt, and kept warm by the heat of his bare chest. With his other hand he clutched a buffalo robe closely around them. The horse didn't need any guidance from him. The baby's lips searched his chest until she found his nipple, but Reuben did not like that, and of course there was nothing to be found there, anyway. Instead, he held a strip of buffalo jerky to her lips and let her suck on that. She was hungry, but it appeared to soothe her.

Reuben had held foals and calves and lambs in his arms, even a cougar kitten and a bear cub, but never a human this small, and rarely a human at all. Women and children had not been part of his life, but he was strange only insofar as it was his need for solitude that kept him away from others. He disliked few people; nonetheless, he entertained few of them and courted none. Reuben Moon had lived through more than two hundred seasons and knew things you couldn't know otherwise. If you came to see him he was pleased enough to see you, but was also glad when you left. Then the silence settled in, and when it did he could put his ear to the ground and hear larvae under the earth and worms burrow through the soil. He would put his face to the wind and search for scents that interested him. He might fly with the birds and look down upon the tops of trees. He was not a shaman and never pretended to be, but still people came with their dreams and asked for mixtures that cured things, and listened when he told them to plant with the waxing moon.

Reuben's mother was a Mescalero Apache and his father a *cibolero*, a New Mexican buffalo hunter. Both were dead by the time he was eight, his mother from cholera and his father from a Comanche lance when the *ciboleros* impinged on their territory. His father had migrated north out of Mexico to follow the still undiminished herds of bison that wandered down from the plains. The *ciboleros* were excellent horsemen and deadly hunters who wielded lances with uncanny accuracy. When not in use these lances were placed butt end into leather cups that were attached by thongs to the pommels of the saddles, and rode straight up with their killing ends in the air. These men banded together in October, when it was cooler and the hides were thickest, and headed north and west across the *llana estacado* into Texas, then north again into what would become Oklahoma.

The hunt which ended in his father's death was Reuben Moon's first. The boy rode abreast of the hunters, but at a safe distance from the herd, and watched them race their horses alongside the beasts and drive their lances deep into their hearts. Then they jumped from their horses, worked the lances free, remounted, and took off again. A good hunter could take twenty to twenty-five buffalo over a three-mile course, and Reuben's father was a good hunter. The *ciboleros* had devised an immense wagon that was capable of hauling a cargo of eighty buffalo carcasses. The morning the Comanche attacked, there were ten fully loaded rigs spread out over the distance of a mile. Six hundred attackers swarmed from the surrounding hills and broke off into elements that circled each wagon, kept them isolated one from the other, and slaughtered those who tried to defend them.

Reuben was the only one left alive. He watched a warrior with a blue face ram a lance through his father's back, punching out pieces of his heart that remained stuck and fluttering on the tip. The warrior jumped from his horse and withdrew the lance from his father's body. The Comanche turned and saw the boy, who was crouched in a fighting position with a skinning knife in his hand; he sneered and backed the boy against the wagon wheel with the lance at his throat. Reuben was ready to die. He locked eyes with his murderer. Other warriors came over—three, four, five of them—all with their lances touching his breast. Their faces were yellow and blue and green, painted with bolts of white lightning, stars, and black circles. The parts they all wore down the middle of their heads were gaudy, too. They stood with their lances touching his breast until the warrior who killed his father grunted something and the others backed away.

Another grunt and two warriors he hadn't seen before, older than he was, but not by much, stepped forward with their lances ready to gut him if ordered, but they were only put there to guard him while the others stripped the corpses and confiscated the wagons. Buzzards already circled overhead, so this happened quickly. When all the Comanche climbed on board the giant rigs and took the reins, the warrior who'd killed his father waved Reuben's guards aside and crouched opposite him with a war club in his hand. Reuben didn't understand what the man said to him and slashed out as he closed in, but the warrior had experience where Reuben had none, and brought the war club down on the boy's knife hand, crunching his wrist and causing him to drop the knife. Another instant and he was put down. The warrior with the blue face held him on the ground and tore off his shirt while the two younger ones stripped him of his trousers and underwear. Naked, his hands were bound behind his back and a rope was placed around his neck, with the other end tied behind one of the wagons. The wagons lurched forward, and from that moment on Reuben Moon was slave to the Comanche.

Reuben Moon
Comanche Territory
1792

EXCEPT FOR WINTER, WHEN HE WAS ALLOWED TO WEAR A
buffalo robe, Reuben was kept naked. All Comanche boys
his age were, but in their ninth year they dressed in breech
cloths and began their grooming as warriors, while Reuben
stayed naked and was forced to do woman's work. He did not
like it, and did nothing he was asked to do until he was asked
to do it again. Even then, he often got a willow switch across
his bare legs, though just as often he dodged and the switch
cut through air with a whistle. They could beat him 'til their
arms dropped. Still, he would not do woman's work. They
could find their own grains and berries. He would not do it.
He would not chew their hides or tan them. He would not stir
their food, and he would not remain naked. He wrapped a
tattered deer hide around himself and held it there with a
braided leather rope. If he had been a grown man, the
Comanche would have tortured and skinned him, then
burned him alive from the feet up, but he was still a boy. His
small fists could sting a grown man but couldn't knock one
down, though when he fought back—which he always did—
it was like you set the devil loose. It was too punishing, even
to win. By and by, they accepted his presence and left him
alone. He remained an enigma. They could not love him, but
his heart astonished them. He remained on the edges of the
tribe, sleeping where he dropped, taking food where he found
it, sometimes straight from the cook pots, sometimes from
scraps thrown to dogs. He was a fixture who belonged nowhere

and to no one. It was not his nature to skulk or hide, and so he walked about where and when he wanted, but never with anybody else, never with anybody at all. They called him Cloud, and his place was with the horses.

——⊶⊷——

They could call him what they wanted, but in his heart Reuben was the name given by his father. The horses knew the truth, and that was what mattered. His place was with the herd. They became his day and his night. He could ride any one of them, and at night chose a brood mare with a broad back on which to sleep. He hung over her neck for warmth, and if a chill set in he tented himself over with a buffalo robe. Comanche horsemanship was legendary deep into Mexico, but Reuben's reputation overrode them all. Word spread through the Comanche community that there was a boy among them with the blood of a horse in his veins. They began taking him on raids, and teaching him what they knew best: war and stealing horses. Their method was to travel in smaller bands to a preordained location and form into the attack party there. They perfected the sudden attack and retreat with separate parties using separate routes, and dividing into ever-diminishing groups as necessary in order to impede pursuit. They receded like waves from the shore. It was as if they were never there.

His job was to follow the warriors with a string of horses, and be ready with a fresh mount when one was needed. They trusted his judgment, and no horse of his suggestion ever gave out under its rider. He could sew up the wounds of a horse, as well as those of a man. He tended to torn flesh with a seriousness of purpose that willed it closed, and it got so that no expedition was undertaken without him. He was ten when he stole his first horse, slipping out of the Comanche camp while the raiding party slept, and sneaking into the herd to be stolen, leaping upon a big horse's back, and hanging on with his hands twisted in its mane as it whirled like a dervish and tried to run out from under him. But Reuben took it where he wanted, and led the other forty-nine out of the defile from a pocket in the rocks where the Chiricahua, who had previously stolen the herd from a military outpost below the border in Mexico, had confined them.

His fourth spring as a captive, he cut open the belly of a living mare to free her foal. She was a paint, like much of the herd, paints being preferred by the Comanche horsemen. She went down at dusk, but the moon came out and she still hadn't delivered. Her swollen stomach heaved with each labored breath. She was a dainty maiden, nervous and dancey, way too small for the great stallion that mounted her every day for weeks nearly a year ago. She had taken an unusually long time to begin foaling, and now that she was down she was down for way too long. She rolled and kicked the air, and that wasn't good. Her water had burst, yet no front hooves had appeared, no nose, no other sign that anything inside that mare was moving.

He lashed her hind legs together and thrust his arm inside her. There were no hooves where there should have been, no nose. He thrust his other arm inside her, too, and with both hands felt for wherever the foal might be. He could feel it now: what he took to be its rump, jammed sideways. It hadn't left the birth canal, was still inside the sac. It might even be on its back. It might even be dead.

The mare was dying, but he did not have time for her to die because her foal would surely suffocate and die, too. Both dead. What good? Wisdom said save the mare, sacrifice the foal, dismember it inside its mother's womb, but too much had burst inside her from the strain of her delivery and she would never pass that foal. She would die with it inside her body, and soon after that the foal would die, too. The mare grunted, and a shiver ran the course of her spine, but her eyes were still clear. If he'd had a lance he'd have placed it over her heart and pushed with his whole weight, but he had no lance, only a knife, sharp enough to slice a hair in half, yes, but not long enough to reach her heart.

His hands knew what to do before his brain did. He tied the mare's front feet together and slit her belly down the center from sternum to womb, scuttled out of the way of her feeble kicks, and, when they stopped, reached in with both his hands and lifted out the foal as if it were an offering. He peeled back the sac and let the head of the small, wet thing rest in his lap where, now on its own, it gulped its first breath of air. Reuben was the first living thing the colt saw. Its eyes lingered on his as if to make certain of something, then it pushed itself from his lap and tried to stand on legs too bony and too long to hold. Its front two splayed out side to side, and its hind parts never made it off the ground at all. The colt, all legs, toppled over, but right off gathered those legs and gave itself a determined push and righted itself, but still couldn't stand. Three legs seemed to work fine, but the fourth went its own way and sent the colt's whole kit 'n' caboodle crashing down again.

A cloud passed over the moon leaving very little light by which to see, and that was when the lacerating cry of a mountain lion ruptured the peace of the evening. Until then, the herd had done little more than acknowledge the birth if, in fact, they even did that, but when the cat cried out—it was as if a current shot through the herd—when the cat cried out the nearby horses surged into a circle around Reuben and the new-born colt. A few days ago a panther had taken a foal from the outskirts of the herd, but Reuben knew from the wall of horses surrounding him that this colt was safe. An old brood-mare bent over the colt, licked him clean, and nuzzled his butt until his hind legs stood him up. The colt staggered, but this time he stayed on his feet. He took a few steps then staggered again, but still he stayed up.

He was a handsome colt with muscular haunches and a broad chest. The moon was out again, and Reuben could see the colt clearly as it stood there. Pure white, except for his tail and all four feet, which were slick black. But what set this horse apart from all the others was that its beautiful broad chest was black, too, like a shield, as were its ears and the top of its head to just below the eyes. Reuben had heard these horses talked about—how they had magic properties, how the warrior who rode one would be protected from harm in battle—but he had never seen one. Its markings had to be exact, and the colt's markings were just that: a black shield and a magic hat. Reuben rubbed the palms of his hands on the sticky nipples of the dead mare and cupped them under the colt's nose. It nuzzled the boy's hands, then licked them clean and followed as they led her to the ripe nipple of the dead mare. The colt snorted, licked it, and began sucking while Reuben stood aside and watched. It stopped for a minute to look back at him, made some kind of noise, and then continued to suck.

As dawn came on, Reuben sensed a disturbance in the herd and wondered if the lion was about. The colt had allowed the boy to run his hands gently over its head and neck and flanks. For a period of time now, he slept while the boy rested his hands on him, but the colt started awake as he, too, sensed a shiver in the herd. The old mare nudged the colt to his feet and stood next to him as the wall of horses parted, and a buckskin mare, heavy with milk, entered the circle, and stopped beside him. The brood mare nudged the colt towards the buckskin's teats, and watched with Reuben as he began to suck.

Reuben named the colt Moon, and claimed it for his own.

At first, when they saw the carcass of the dead mare, what had been done to it, the Indians were angry enough to gut Reuben, too, but when they saw what had been born they stood in wonder. Word spread. Cloud birthed a magic horse! Cloud did this thing! Cloud! Cloud!

No. No!

He knew his name, and his name was Reuben Moon. *You call me that! You and you! All of you! My name is Reuben Moon!*

By the time the young horse was strong enough to ride, he had become so accustomed to the weight of Reuben Moon that when the boy sat him for the first time the moment came and went without a squabble. The young horse gave no notice that there was anything out of the ordinary, but on its back Reuben felt invincible.

The time came when he dreamed in Comanche, heard the words and knew them, because now they were his as well. In his dream he wore the blue hip-high riding boots of the Comanche warrior and black face paint—a band of black across the eyes and a second across the cheeks and nose. He had been adopted into the tribe and in Comanche fashion wandered with them, as they always did, on horseback in battle formation. But he never forgot the sight of his father's heart quivering on the point of a Comanche lance.

Esau Burdock
New Orleans, Louisiana
November 18, 1833

ESAU BURDOCK SAT ON THE BALCONY OF HIS HOTEL ROOM overlooking the street, with his muddy boots up on the wrought iron railing. It was 10 p.m. and black. The stars were fiery pellets flung across the sky by the fistful. He was tired, but couldn't close his eyes for the show. He'd seen these showers before—every year, in fact—but all of them were pale beside this one. People were taking note of it. Some wondered if it were the end of the world. One heard wails and lamentations, but one also heard horns and exclamations of wonder. The entire state of Louisiana was fixed and in its thrall. Not even the blind could look away.

He had come down the Missouri River to pick up a stallion shipped from Kentucky for the wild herd he was grooming back in New Mexico. The western ponies were agile and quick and had great endurance, but the stallion would bring size and strength to the herd. Burdock had always liked New Orleans and looked forward to his few days in the city, even though he was almost hanged there as a young man. That wasn't the first time he risked a hanging, either.

Burdock, was oversized and ruddy, even from birth fifty plus years ago to a common criminal in an alleyway in London. He nearly split his mother in two while he fought his way out. Her natural hair was nearly white, but his was thick and red; he still had most of it, augmented now by a full red beard. The only thing his mother taught him before she died was how to pick a man's pocket. He never knew his father, nor did she. Pretty near as soon as the boy could stand, she taught him to toddle up to a likely prospect and hang onto a man's sleeve until the man gave him a coin or shook him off. While Esau had the man distracted, his mother lifted the wallet from his pocket. This gambit continued to work until her fingers twisted with arthritis and bony knobs stood out on her gnarled wrists. It got so that she barely left her old straw mattress for the pain. Esau stole whatever he could whenever he could, to get them through a dreadful winter. He'd stalk the back streets looking for drunks, and if they were passed out he'd swipe everything in their pockets. If they weren't passed out, but only staggering, he learned that hitting them over the head with a lead pipe more than made up for a victim's strength and stature. If the man were very tall Esau would bang him on the ankle, and then, when he bent down to clutch it, crack him hard over the head.

She'd been feeling a little better for a while, Esau's mother, when she suggested they try a new gambit. She would hang onto the gentlemen's coat sleeves herself, and Esau would pick their pockets. "Teaching you a skill they won't hang you for," she said about her lessons to him. He remembered what his mother's hands had looked like and how they moved, as gracefully as a fish through water, how they slipped so easily in and out of a gentleman's pocket. His hands were like mallets compared to hers, so he wasn't as confident as she was that he could do this, but he'd give it a try, add it to his repertoire. His mother had become so hideous he didn't doubt but that she'd be a monstrous distraction as long as she kept hold of a gentleman's coat.

She clutched a fistful of Esau's sleeve as she shuffled along beside him on their way to a busy street she knew to be full of easy scores. Her breath was repellent but it was worse back in their room, where even turned to the wall he couldn't get away from it. Once on the street she spotted a prospect quickly, winked at Esau like she'd found the Grail, and hitched her head in the mark's direction. She let go of Esau's sleeve, and with another hitch of her head bid him follow her until he was on one side of the unsuspecting pigeon and she was on the other.

With a "Please, sir" that came out like a shriek, she grabbed the man's sleeve in both her hands and begged him to help a sick, old lady. Esau hadn't yet seen an opening. The man was horrified and struggled to get away from her, but she shrieked and hung on and dropped to her knees, dragging the man off balance and on top of her as she pitched forward into the street. A passerby would have seen a young man helping a gentleman disentangle himself from a stricken beggar woman. He would have heard another passerby shout, "My God, she's dead!" when the woman remained where she fell like a heap of rags and bones, and he would have heard the gentleman yell for a constable. The young man had answered, "Yes, sir!" so it was assumed he had gone for that same constable. In fact, he was at the outer edge of the gawking crowd and picked three more pockets before he faded back into the depths of the city. That night he slept in a room he paid for, and never gave the one he had shared with his mother another thought.

———— ∞∞∞ ————

Esau lived by his wits on the streets of London: a dodger. He had absolutely no compunction whatsoever about doing anything illegal the instant the opportunity presented itself. He had the primal instincts for a quick score. By the time the boy was fourteen, there wasn't a crime he hadn't committed. He didn't precisely know if he'd murdered anyone; some of those gentlemen had been whopped over the head pretty hard. In a contest between a lead pipe and a skull, the skull comes in second.

He was a master petty criminal, but he aspired to more. In stature he had grown to be quite large (not so easy to dodge 'em anymore), and his ambitions had grown as well. He aspired to improve his class, an impossibility that no amount of custom tailoring and fine dining could breach. Money could not buy class, and his fury at this injustice made his street attacks more savage. But, here's the irony. He could not stop himself from picking a pocket if the pocket presented itself; he was never above emptying the poor box in the church; he was not beyond filching coins from a blind beggar's cup. Esau Burdock could not resist a crime no matter how small, and that's why he got his break, although at the time it didn't seem like any luck at all. All he did was nick a daisy off a flower girl's cart. The woman went berserk and bashed him with her watering can, at which he bashed her back, then put his pie-sized hands around her throat and would have killed her hadn't a constable broken his nightstick across Esau's head. Fate gave him back a bit of his own. It also offered him a choice: hang for theft and attempted murder, or indenture himself and be on the next ship to America.

He signed on with a man who might have been even meaner than he was. He was a slave trader heading back to New Orleans who had been in London to personally negotiate X number of shipments of human cargo to the United States and the West Indies. He had a good eye for a bargain and purchased six young African males on the spot, fit and strong, but their anger showed. Prime stock, but they had to be broken and would be; then one could reasonably expect many productive years out of them. Sometimes men like these try to starve themselves to death if there is no other way to die. It would be Esau's job to see that they arrived in America fit for the marketplace. If any of them died, Esau would get the blame and a nasty beating. "Do not hit them in the face," his master cautioned Esau with a finger on his chest. "And no scars across the back. The buyer will think the black buck is trouble."

When they went on a hunger strike this is what he did: He only beat one of them, and he let the others watch, let them watch as he forced a red hot coal between the slave's clenched teeth, and what was worse let them hear the man die in little bits, hear the man beg to die. "Please, let me die," in his own language. "Please, let me die." His meaning clear. Still, no marks showed on his body, but his insides had burst from the pounding, and he was bleeding to death where it couldn't be seen. Esau had been methodical. Death was slow and agonizing, death by design, meant to reduce a man who was already nothing to a whimpering pulp. At the end of the voyage Esau delivered four healthy males. Losing a percentage of your stock was not an unexpected expense, so he got his ear boxed but received no beating. He was learning the rules.

Esau Burdock
New Orleans
1791

THE SLAVE PENS OF NEW ORLEANS STOOD IN A PART OF THE city not usually traveled by polite society, where shooting galleries, betting dens, cock fights, sex parlors, and saloons pockmarked the streets. The pens were bounded on the street side by high brick walls. Inside were large courtyards where the slave children ran free, separate sleeping quarters for men and women, and a trading room where auctions were held and deals struck. There were curtained nooks around the room where the slaves were made to strip while being more closely examined, though the stock was often displayed outside, lined up neatly in new blue suits and calico dresses. A gentleman went there to do business or not at all.

Esau Burdock saw profit here. Basil Hunt, the man to whom he was bound, put him to work as general factotum at his establishment: *Hexley, Harlow & Hunt—Purveyors of Negroes*. For the first time in his life, Esau knew he could thrive and grow profit. He would watch, and he would learn. The four surviving Negroes shipped from London brought word of his brutality into the slave pen, where it spread immediately among the stock already there. No one challenged Esau Burdock. They feared him before he ever set foot in the door.

∞∞∞

Young Burdock embraced his work, not because he had any particular distaste for Negroes, but because he saw a means to improve his station. He noted the fine clothes the owners wore, their fancy carriages, their wine imported from France. They were businessmen who did business with other wealthy men, important men whose affairs shaped the way for them all. For the time being, he would step lively and do what was asked. He ran errands and kept the place clean, and he did whatever was ordered to keep the stock in good condition. When he started off he was on the low rung of the ladder, but that was better than being a Negro, because a Negro didn't have no rung at all. There wasn't no place a darky could go, but he could go, Esau Burdock could go, and he would. This was a new country, and he aimed to make his mark on it.

Esau was first up in the morning and had the stock washed, fed, dressed, and ready for viewing by the time the partners came in. The bucks were dressed in identical blue suits, ties, and top hats. Each skivvy was given a new calico dress and head wrap. Little children ran naked. Older children wore rags that barely kept them modest, and their mothers were made to coat their bodies with oil that made their skin glisten. Esau made them smile and gave them a peanut when they did, sometimes a grape. The mothers groomed their children as best they could. It was common knowledge that the better they looked, and the better they behaved, the better the chance that the buyer would take the entire family.

Burdock brought his own peculiar cunning to the slave market, and later, as he continued to learn, to the trade itself. In the beginning he slept in the same room as them, but they were chained and he was not. He ate with them, too, ate the same corn mush he poured in their troughs twice a day, though he sat straight up in a chair, ate his with a spoon off a plate, not with his fingers. Mid-morning, and again in the middle of the afternoon, he got all of them on their feet in the main yard—old women, children, every one—and had them dance and sing for exercise. It was the god damnedest sight: all those Ethiopes dancing and singing, and most of them with tears streaming down their faces, some of them moaning, and who would want to hear that? So he asked them one morning who could play the fiddle, and when he saw there were two hands up he went to Mr. Hunt and asked him could he find him a used fiddle? Hunt laughed when Esau told him what for, but he listened as the boy assured him it was good for the stock and would be reflected in the prices they brought. The music would lift their spirits and keep them moving. It also drowned out the moans. Force was a way, and he had no hesitation when it was, but it was not the only way. This came to him early on. Besides, the whip left marks, and a slave with a scarred back would be seen as trouble, and thus harder to sell.

Esau came to know the product better than the men who owned it. He felt no pity for them, but he felt no hatred either. They were slaves. Providence had handed them that as surely as it landed him here, but it still left him with the ability to determine his own fate. For these others, their fate was some master's whimsy. They would die unknown, and he would not. He was working out his destiny. Everything he'd done until now had brought him to this place, and Providence put the Negroes in his hands. They were his to make the best of, his means of stepping up, and he watched out for his opportunities. Landing in New Orleans was one of them.

He despised England. It was already thousands of years old when he was born—a dirty, tight, cramped little country. But New Orleans was young and bursting outwards. There had been a fire that burnt to cinders the wooden buildings and pike fence that the first Frenchmen built, and the new structures of brick and white plaster glowed on sunny days and glistened in the rain. It was finally a part of the United States. The streets were filled with bluster and dreams. They teemed with the babel of nations, with exiles nobody wanted at home—convicts, the homeless, prostitutes, all swept up and put on ships—all, except the Choctaws here for centuries, from someplace else. The French and Spanish influences were everywhere, from the architecture and food to the Creole beauties and Acadian octoroons who were envied by so many. There was a German colony of 2,000 just north, brought here by the French a few years earlier. The streets actually made his mouth water, so he relished the chance to run an errand outside the pen. He'd buy some tobacco off a Choctaw, pounded and mixed with sumac and sweet gum, and dally on his errands to spend more time in the streets. It seemed to Esau Burdock that you could buy anything in these streets if you had money. Even without money you felt part of the riches.

In London there was nothing to look at. In New Orleans he never wanted to close his eyes, never wanted to sleep for long in case something from the street circus walked by, in case an inkling of some strange food nicked his curiosity. His life 'til now had been all fish 'n' chips and mush, but here it could be custard, a new one every day, bolstered with the morning's cream and eggs not one hour old.

Once out of the pen and on the street, a man got a different picture of things. In London people always looked as if they were resigned to being hanged. Not here. Not even the Negroes, not even when the weather was hot. The ones here in New Orleans worked as coopers, draymen, carpenters, cooks, blacksmiths, side by side with their masters. Negroes were everywhere, some of them free, nearly so many of them as whites. And everyone, African and white, seemed to have a purpose. There was work completed by the end of the day, something one could see and hold in the hand. There was money to be made with skilled slaves trained to do such things. Mr. Hunt had taught him to read from a book written by a doctor, where he learned how smoothly the mechanism of the universe runs and functions when everything is in its ordained place. This was a universal truth: The true nature of the Negro was to be subservient. The disposition of Africans remained cheerful when occupied productively, well fed, and reasonably housed, without those worries of sustenance that were the white man's concern, and better left to it. Tend the Negroes like a garden, and they will bring sustenance to all.

Thus Esau Burdock formed his opinions.

One morning he found himself on an errand that took him by the docks. A fine rain was passing through. He stopped and watched a gang of dusky hands offloading provisions from a ship in from the West Indies, mostly sugar, but also indigo, plantains, coffee, and cocoa. They were fine big boys, sturdy and upright, working shirtless, glistening in the mist, muscles bulging under the hundred weight of sugar sacks. Their countenances were active, not the dull and listless expressions of slaves in the pen. Two overseers stood by with whips, but never had need of them. The slaves accepted their work and moved swiftly in great strides, up one gangplank and steadily down the other under a full load. Up the plank. Down the plank. Into the hold. Out of the hold. Tick. Tock. Tick. Tock. Up. Down. In. Out. Tick. Tock. Efficient. Must've been the way the pharaohs did it, how they got those pyramids built. When the Bos'n's whistle piped out, the gang of men stopped work and went to the street at the end of the wharf, where a Choctaw woman stood stirring a thick mix in an iron pot resting on a substantial bed of red coals. Each man took an oblong ball the size of a woman's fist wrapped in shucks from a woven basket—*banaha*, cornmeal boiled and wrapped in the shucks—Choctaw bread. They were allowed to eat however so many they wanted, and, while they did, she filled the proper number of bowls with the soupy hotchpotch ladled from the iron pot.

God damn! These Sambos eat better than me!

Esau learned from the overseers on the dock that they belonged to a wealthy master who got the most out of them by treating them with scientific principles. Other men would work the slaves 'til they dropped, then get some more. Feed 'em mostly mush. But this master made sure his Negroes ate well. That Choctaw woman cooked food like they ate back in Africa: peanuts, greens, yams, okra. It suited them better and so became wisdom. Sometimes these slaves were even allowed to hunt. Meat on the table made a man strong. They worked hard, and sometimes even sang when they worked. After work they went back home to the cabins built for them, and ate supper with their families. You'd hear them singing at night, too. Not the ones in the pen though. Kept a man up the whole goddamn time with their crying.

So Esau looked and Esau listened and Esau learned.

He knew in his heart that he was meant for more than a common pickpocket. It wasn't the criminal nature so much as the pettiness of his crimes that bothered him. However, now here he was in a new life in a new country with new rules, and nothing to stop a man of his determination and enterprise from making a success of himself.

———⚬⚬⚬———

By the third year of his servitude, Esau knew the business as well as the gentlemen who owned it. *Hexley, Harlow & Hunt* was the best managed slave pen in New Orleans. Its stock brought top dollar, in part because Esau knew how to extract every red cent out of a deal, and in part because he applied scientific principles to the trade. He learned early on that a daily diet of bread, corn mush, and strips of salt pork led to a weak and inefficient work force, while slaves fed a diet of native wild greens and other vegetables, even without much meat, stood taller and made a much greater impression on the buyer. As field hands on the plantations they worked longer, more productive days, with fewer injuries and sicknesses. So he rented a small plot of fertile ground from a Choctaw farmer, had the man teach the slaves from the pen to plant Native American crops, and had the slaves teach the Choctaw to grow foods native to the Africans: rice, *tania*, *eddo*, cassava, and watermelon, too. Progressive owners had their Negroes plant watermelon in between the rows of corn, so that on hot days they could refresh themselves in the fields. It was a great favorite.

———⚬⚬⚬———

Esau Burdock was nothing if not canny, as shrewd as an
urchin who had worked the feral streets of London could be.
Subtleties of movement, vague implications, words unspoken–
none of these were lost on him. He assessed the strengths and
weaknesses of his chattel just as he assessed the strengths and
weaknesses of his clientele, and what he discerned was this:
The key factor in selling a Negro was to get the Negro to sell
himself. You had to be smart about this and first take the
measure of the sale. Could be a man got sold without his wife
and pleaded with his new master to buy her, too, then she had
to convince the master that she was worth the bargain. What
was he looking for? A cook? Seamstress? Wet nurse? "Yes,
mars, I kin do dat." Then the master would look at the length
of her fingers to see if they were nimble enough to pick cotton, or take her behind a curtain to check her breasts to see if
they were full, pull up her skirt and inspect for scars and disease, and was she still capable of bearing children? Could be a
woman was sold without her husband, then he'd have to convince the mars to take him, too. Was his wife's new master in
the market for a cooper or a blacksmith or a slave regal enough
to open the front door for guests? If the trader knew what the
buyer was looking for he'd convey that information to the
Negro, directly, indirectly, whatever was needed. The Negro
could say to his wife's new master, "Yessuh, Mars, I kin for
sure drive dat carriage to town," whether he could or not he
said it to sell himself. But, later, when the new master discovered that his brand new coon couldn't drive a dog cart let
alone a carriage, well, that coon got whupped but good.
Sometimes the master be so mad he'd take a bull whip to him
then rub salt and vinegar into his raw wounds the next day.
Any time after that if a potential purchaser wanted to see was
he a troublesome buck or not, all he'd have to do was look at
the scars on the slave's back. As far as the trader was concerned,

a deal was a deal, and he wasn't going to take no burr-head back.

In the end, of course, it was the buyer's decision. Esau had closed a deal on a little boy, about six, light skinned and smart, perfect for a house servant, possibly even to train as a valet. His mother, who was heavily pregnant, begged to be sold with him, but the buyer would have none of her, paid a handsome price for the boy, said she'd have another one soon enough, and carried him off to Mississippi. Well, hell, the woman would not stop wailing. Nothing could get her to quiet down. Screamed and cried so awful. The noise drove customers out of the show room. The Negroes were agitated, too, starting to talk up and back, singing a song to say goodbye to the boy. Esau gave the woman a shovel and told her to dig a big hole. When she had, he made her lie down with her swollen belly in the hole, tied her hands over her head, and whipped her until she passed out.

A slave could also squelch his own sale by coming up with a limp or talking stupid. Maybe the buyer's reputation in the slave pen was as a cruel man. No slave wanted to be bought by him, so they'd stoop like they were old or come up with an ailment to spoil the sale, a weak arm or a cough, act feeble, something.

You get to know what to look for.

By the fifth year of his servitude, Esau had mastered the trade. His skill at his labors more than paid off for his masters at *Hexley, Harlow, & Hunt,* two of whom were now dead, and the third, Mr. Hexley, so debilitated by a stroke that his wife left much of the company's daily operation to Esau. Most of the previous year he'd spent driving a slave coffle to the Mississippi cotton fields, the killing fields, those dreaded more than any other by the slaves. But for Esau it was a change of pace, having spent his life so far strictly in the city.

He'd never before seen such excellent houses, those on the great plantations of the Deep South. Palatial structures, impeccably white, with soaring columns, wide verandas, great, green lawns, and oak-lined drives leading to elegant front entrances too grand to be considered mere doors. Esau knew from what the slaves talked about among themselves that inside those mansions were crystal chandeliers and parqueted ballrooms, graceful stairways that swooped from one polished landing to another, smokehouses filled with hundreds of hams, larder for a thousand people, slaves as sleek as their masters' horses. Living outside on the road like he did, Esau looked little better than the stock he drove, and so he had never been inside one, even had to endure the indignity of a house servant telling him to go 'round by the back door.

But Esau had come to think of himself as an essential cog in a complex economy, a skilled businessman in a very difficult business, and he wasn't about to let anyone skin him of his dignity. He'd go head to head haggling with the planters, and he wouldn't back down, acted like he didn't care one bit if he walked away from a sale, considered his stock a damn sight more valuable than most, and wouldn't settle for less than market worth. But when the bargaining was done, Esau knew to make certain he left the buyer feeling like he was a man of wealth and power. These men measured their worth by their slaves. It was a constant source of discussion among them—current market prices, the plus and minus of buying light skinned Negroes, breeding as a means of increase—they talked about these and other matters relating to their Negroes incessantly. What a man thought of himself and what other men thought of him depended upon the slaves he owned. Esau knew this and used it to his advantage. He left the buyer thinking he was still champion after a hard fought, hard won fight.

———∞∞∞———

Esau Burdock found this new land a place of promise. He soon divined that an enterprising man, if he looked sharp, could truly make something of himself. His bondage had been to the streets of London, and no doubt he would have died there had luck not plucked him from the gibbet and plunked him smack in the middle of the largest and most successful Negro market in the United States. This was the fuel firing the burgeoning economy and political power of the South, and the supply was endlessly renewable—stretching all the way from tribal warfare in central Africa through Arab and Portugese slavers to the hands of Esau Burdock in New Orleans. It was the first real opportunity life had handed him, and Esau sought to make the most of it. The coffle was a way to manage his own outfit without supervision and sharpen his skills under difficult circumstances, and the side money he'd make through short-term rentals as they passed through settlements would go a long way to paying off his own indenture. He'd been running a short-term rental operation out of the market itself—all known to his employers, of course—and the income from these rentals (a wench to help cook for a wedding, a buck to unload the goods and stock the shelves) all but covered the cost of feeding the entire pen for a month.

Esau put together a caravan of fifty Negroes taken from *Hexley, Harlow, & Hunt,* as well as from two other local slave markets looking to ease up their inventories. Able-bodied men were first in line, two by two, manacled and chained together. They were followed by women who walked with their walking age children, and then by wagons in which rode women who were pregnant, the elderly brought to cook and tend camp, as well as the sick and injured. Esau bought himself traveling clothes, naval trousers from a ship's store and a used French army jacket in fine shape except for the bullet-hole in the back, and stuffed into his belt an old .75 caliber English boarding pistol with a barrel opening the size of a Bermuda shilling. He rode horseback with three other mounted overseers, each armed with guns and carrying whips. And, of course, there were two Negro fiddlers leading the procession. Esau set out just before planting season, and planned to be on the road up to three months as he drove his coffle the 268 miles to market in Natchez, Mississippi.

Basically, he treated the slaves in the coffle no different than he had in the pen, maybe with a little more discipline because, after all, he did have a responsibility to keep them moving. Nevertheless, Esau knew himself to be a fair man: Obey him and you'd be all right. He continued to believe in making an example of one to avoid punishing all the others. The right example would terrify an entire coffle into submission, and the second week out on the road handed him the opportunity for such an example.

They camped one night beside a river, intending to cross it in the morning. The men's hands were freed, though their feet remained chained together. Women, children, and old people were allowed to walk around. There was little worry that they would escape, and if they did, the gang of men paid to apprehend runaways would soon bring them back. They were called "patrollers" and hunted slaves with dogs. Any slave caught off his master's boundaries without a pass would get a beating so severe he would live out the rest of his life as a cripple, if he lived at all. No one ran, but one man did kill another. A big man turned on a little man and strangled him, and that act of murder had to be dealt with. Some of these people did not fear death—in fact, preferred it to servitude, so the death punishment was often desired. The murderer was one of those, a man of middle age who would look on death as a gift. What to do?

Esau ordered the overseers to unchain the man's feet and put the manacles back on his wrists. Then he ordered the corpse of the murdered man to be tied on the back of his murderer. Everywhere the man walked he carried his victim with him. You could see he would rather have died. Fluid leaked from the dead man's mouth onto his murderer's neck. The man screamed and moaned, rocked back and forth, fell to the ground, tried to scrape the dead man off. Fear ran the length of the coffle like shivers down a beast's back. Fear of the dead that clung to his murderer. Fear of the beast about to devour them. Fear that the cudgels of the dead would beat them senseless. Death rode the killer like a pony. He got to his knees, stretched his hands the full length of their chain, and fell dead.

———— ∞ ————

The rest of the way to Natchez went without incident.

———— ∞ ————

Natchez, Mississippi, the royal seat of King Cotton, sat up on a bluff overlooking the blue brown river. Local boosters brayed about it, the territorial capital of the Mississippi Territory, a place already swelling with wealth, its arms wide open for more. Its position on the river was such that plantations with a thousand slaves brought their cotton to be loaded onto boats, then shipped down river to New Orleans, and from there to the textile mills in England. However, this would soon change. The steamboat would change it, and the appearance of that invention, only a short few years away, meant that the planters would be able to ship their bales up river to the textile mills of the North instead of shipping them across the ocean. Natchez was already counting its money, and its slave market, Forks of the Road, had quickly become the second largest market for Negroes in the United States. Only New Orleans surpassed it.

Before the French had annihilated them in retaliation for a massacre of French citizens, the Natchez Indians were slave traders themselves, often joining forces with the Yazoo and Chickasaw on far-ranging raids, then selling their captives to the English as slave labor to work the sugar plantations in the West Indies. The massacre at Fort Rosalie was well deserved, but ruthless. The Natchez sent word to the French plantations that the African slaves should join them. Many did, as did Yazoo, Chickasaw, Choctaw, and Illinois. Pregnant women had their bellies ripped open. Nursing children were killed, and then their mothers. Hundreds of men were slaughtered, and hundreds more women and children were taken as slaves. When Esau got there, what was left of the Natchez was scattered among a hat-full of lesser Indian tribes, but the traffic in Negroes was expected to increase a thousand fold once steamboats began to chug upstream.

———— ∞∞∞ ————

Esau entered Natchez from the south, and drove the coffle north and east through the streets of town towards Forks of the Road's eastern border. His horse had given out some miles back, so he traded with a Yazoo farmer and walked the rest of the way at the head of the column with that canteen of whiskey rarely far from his lips. He wasn't about to dance, but he felt like it. Esau told the fiddlers, "Play a lively tune!"

The homes they passed were palatial, considered by their owners to be the equal of any in the world. These men were planters who lived with their families atop the Natchez bluff for safety, but owned and worked property across the river in

Louisiana. The coffle, what was left of it, was rag tag and mot-ley, mostly older ones, and some couple of 'em sick. Except for an occasional dunk in the river, nobody bathed in the three months they'd been on the road. People turned away in dis-gust as the caravan passed, and Esau felt something for per-haps the only time in his life: embarrassed. He was as filthy as his Negroes, with the animal smell of the coffle on him. He wanted nothing more than to burn his clothing and soak in a tub of hot, soapy water. And to eat.

The slave market was situated on the spot about a mile east of town where three roads came together. Once inside the wide wooden gate the market was a sprawl of small wooden buildings, holding pens, tents, and stands containing hun-dreds of slaves tended by the traders and those in their employ. Livestock was for sale, as well. Negroes were not auctioned here. Prospective buyers roamed freely and shopped at their leisure, then negotiated quietly with the sellers when they had made their decisions. When a buyer settled on a purchase, no money changed hands. Instead, paper notes from buyer to seller spelled out the terms of payment and rate of interest. Together with the sum he had amassed by keen and clever trading on the route north, Esau would deliver a small fortune to his employers. He told his overseers see to it that the Negroes were cleaned, clothed, fed, and readied for sale as soon as possible. Finally, he made certain his men understood that the Louisiana guarantee, a money back provision, was not applicable here. Then Esau gave the overseers their pay plus expenses, and said see you in the morning.

Natchez-Under-The-Hill was as raw as the mansions on the bluff above were refined. Here ships took on cargos of Africans and cotton bound for sale or shipment down river. Esau knew he couldn't get through the front doors of those grand houses, but the doors down below—doors where a man could place a bet, get a drink, watch a fight (or start one), and enjoy the attention of a sinful woman—those doors were wide open. It was a rambunctious place, and Esau Burdock was in a rambunctious frame of mind. He didn't remember when he'd ever felt so free. But here, now, he was a young man loose in the city with nobody to please, and money in his pocket to spend when he got there.

Hungry as he was, feeling filthy felt worse. He tried an inn at the river's edge that promised board, a bath, and a bed, but it turned out that bed was in a room with twelve other beds, and Esau thought he'd rather sleep outside standing up than pay for that. Back on the street he passed a stand with a sign stating *Public Wash* in white letters on a red field with a blue border. Two lines of fresh laundry flapped down either side of the rickety building, little more than a shack, really, but clean. A woman—a prune, black, wrinkled, and very small—used a wooden paddle to stir the clothes boiling in a cauldron that hung from a tripod over a fire pit in front of the building. Esau took her for a free Negro, until the old woman explained that it was her eldest daughter, Princess, bought herself and now she was free and has this business. The girl rents her mother and younger sister from Mr. A. Coulter who own them, so they can work here for her. She pays him rent and covers expenses for her sister and her mother, and they all get to live here.

"You got anything I can trade for?" he asked, indicating his clothes. "They're dirty but they ain't torn or nothin'. Wash up good as new."

"Got shot in the back and still standin'?" came a voice from behind him, a woman's voice, direct and kind of jokey. Esau turned and saw a big-boned colored woman, brown as a walnut, standing in the doorway holding a wooden tub full of dirty laundry on one wide hip. Her arms were almost as big as his. He took off his coat and put his fingers through the bullet hole in the back. "You could sew that, right?" he asked, "Make it like new."

"It ain't new."

"Make it like," he said.

"Got somethin' better," she replied.

"What d'ya got?"

She appraised him from the steps and made a little motion for Esau to turn around, which he did. He wasn't comfortable being scrutinized like this.

"One more time," she said, and when reluctantly he did it again, she said, "We could fix you up smart." She carried the washtub of clothes over to the tripod and put it down beside the old woman. "You want some coffee, ma'am?" she asked her mother.

"Mm hm," answered the woman, still stirring the cauldron of boiling clothes. Her mouth was another wrinkle.

"Fix you some," said Princess, and motioned for Esau to follow her into the house.

Inside were piles of clothes—dunes, mountains of them—neatly folded and stacked according to some order; men's clothes, women's clothes, all kind of clothes, and boots in fishing nets hung from the rafters. Esau's were long since wore through, and he could surely use a pair.

"Somethin' in here for everybody," Princess said proudly. "Root around. See what jump out on you." She crossed to the wood stove and poured out two cups of coffee. One she handed to Esau. "Got molasses over to the stove," she said, but he didn't want any. The other she took outside to her mother. He heard them laughing, was certain they were talking about him, and did not like it one bit. "Get the hell back in here," he bellowed through the door. "Take your clothes off and get in the tub," she called back. "You better go on," warned her mother. "Think he own the world, don't he?" said Princess. "Don't he?" her mother said right back.

⸺⸎⸺

Esau still had on every stitch of his clothing when Princess returned from outside. She saw that he was getting edgy and, thinking it best to reassure him, asked his name. She referred to him as *Mr.* Burdock, explained to him with all due respect, *Mr.* Burdock, that clean clothes were ten cents a pound, and he was welcome to try on any and as many for size and fashion, but the city fathers said she had to offer bathing services with no choice but to do it. They don't want nothin' passed on, so . . . She'd said her piece, shrugged, and smiled. "I run a clean business, Mr. Buddock," she added.

"Burdock," he corrected.

"Yessir, Mr. Burdock. We got lots of hot water. Scrub up good."

"Where?" Grumpy. He wasn't going to pretend to like this. Princess pulled aside a yellow calico curtain at one end of the room, revealing an old tin bathtub. She put her hand in the water. "Good 'n' hot," she said.

"I ain't washin' in everybody's dirty water," said Esau.

"It's always clean. I just keep it hot and ready," explained Princess. "No waitin'. This is Mr. Burdock's bath, nobody else. And you're Mr. Burdock, so it's yours."

Something was going on, and it annoyed him mightily, but he couldn't put his finger on what it was, not exactly, but it was something. She seemed to be a good one eager to please. "How much is this going to cost me?" he wanted to know.

"Ten cents a pound for new clothes, five cents gets you the tub for a half hour plus extra, unless somebody else wants to use it, soap a penny, shave three cents, my razor 'cause I can see you ain't got one. Fix you up pretty. Get you lookin' new in no time. Take your clothes off and get in." He hesitated. "Pull the curtain, hand out your clothes, and get in," she explained.

Esau did what she asked, and that hot water felt awful good. It wasn't long before he was asleep.

———— ∞∞∞ ————

Esau Burdock left Princess's place looking like a young man of means. He'd watched those men often at the market in New Orleans casually perusing the stock, twirling their walking sticks, bantering with each other; young men impressed with themselves, sure of their place in the world and bolstered by their family's good fortune. Princess had fed him, too—corn mush and coffee—charged him, of course, but let him eat as much as he could hold. When he asked her was that bed in the corner occupied she said it was, but she'd let him sleep on a pile of clothes. Cost a dollar. "Who sleeps in it?" he asked.

"Me 'n' Mama," said Princess.

"How much?"

"How much for what?"

"The bed," he grinned. "No mama. Just you."

"Thank you for the compliment, sir. Don't think I don't appreciate the thought, but I got too much clothes to clean to bother with that stuff," she said as she indicated the piles around the room with a weary smile. "Good as you look, it'd be wasted on me, anyway, Mr. Buddock . . . "

"Burdock."

"Probably I'd just fall asleep." She came over and roughly, Esau thought, adjusted the frill of his shirt and flattened both lapels, tugged the cuffs of his shirtsleeves so that they showed an inch beyond the sleeves of his coat, turned him around and tugged at its tail, turned him again, and adjusted the way his trousers fell. They were a large plaid, red and yellow, very popular two years back, and matched his gray waistcoat with its black velvet collar. He liked the way he looked, but not the way this woman kept poking and picking at him. He didn't like that at all and finally pushed her hands away. Later, out on the street again, he decided she deserved to be whipped, and if she were his that's what would have happened. He knew she'd done some kind of something to him. Voodoo magic, maybe, but, hell, he didn't have to know what she done, only that she done it. Princess. There's a name for you. Princess. Cheeky bitch.

———— ∞∞∞ ————

She was glad he was gone and hoped he wouldn't come back, but if he did and wanted to sleep on a pile of clothes she'd have to let him. She was well known for offering folks a place to sleep, so she couldn't very well turn him away. Unless he was drunk. Then there would be trouble. He would force himself, and she would fight him off. Her mother would watch, horrified, from the corner. He could kill her. She would not let him have her, and when she could, she'd reach beneath her bed for the rusted bayonet and drive it through his heart.

Then what?

She prayed to God this man would stay away.

Esau Burdock was a young man on the loose for the first time in years. He ambled along the streets of Natchez dressed in the finest clothes he'd ever had, and with all the looks and nods that came his way he felt like an important man, a businessman of some account. First he'd finish up his dealings at Forks of the Road and send the overseers back to New Orleans. If the men wanted, they could put together another coffle to drive south and pick up more cash along the way. They could also float down river or go by steamship, but Esau would return to New Orleans in his own good time. He knew he had to buy another horse. He'd get to that next. Esau would take his time until he found one befitting his stature. He did not know as much about horses as he knew about Negroes, but he knew that a good man on a good horse was someone to reckon with. One day. That such a thing was surely in his future made his heart thump when he considered it.

He bid goodbye to his overseers, left their presence, and immediately became someone more than he was before. He wandered among the stands, stalls, and corrals, his chest out as if he were a man of leisure eager to do only what pleasured him. He observed the sales and trades with a practiced eye. A sleek, black carriage pulled by two matched gray geldings and driven by an elegant Negro in fine livery came to a halt near him. Esau watched as a trader left his stall and ran to help its occupant climb down. It was a barouche, the fanciest carriage of its day, with a fold-up hood at the back and two seats facing each other. Esau wondered what it would be like to ride in one when an idea came to him. It was only an inkling so far, as much in his gut as in his head. He watched as its owner was fawned over by the trader.

The planter, Esau was certain of that, looked like a man who walked the fields himself. The man was short and burly—Esau was a good head taller—but with an air of command. If he were a guard dog you'd know not to go too far. He wore a wide-brimmed floppy leather hat, homespun shirt, and rough weave trousers stuffed into muddy boots. His eyes, large for his head, swiveled in their sockets like search beams, but when they fixed on something they narrowed and focused like the rays of the sun through a magnifying glass. He was twenty years Esau's senior, but still looked to have the power of a barrel-chested strongman in the circus. Esau had once seen one break a chain by expanding his chest, and it looked as if this man could do it, too. His nose showed signs of drink, the only weakness Esau could see.

Esau watched, he thought discreetly, as a line of Negro males was brought out for the planter to see. He walked the line like an inspector general, rejected each one, and asked for more. Another line was quickly trotted out. This time the planter walked back and chose the Negro in the middle.

"I bought your woman a few days ago, didn't I?" asked the planter.

"Yes, suh," answered the slave.

"You miss her?"

"Yes, suh. She and me been together a long time."

"You a good worker like she is?"

"Oh, yes, suh. I can pick all day and all night if the mars want me to."

"You don't, I'll skin you like a snake and nail your hide to the barn door."

"Yes, suh."

"I don't lie."

"No, suh."

"Your woman won't like that."

"No, suh."

The planter turned his eyes on Esau.

"You watchin' all this, friend?" asked the planter.

Esau nodded.

"Well, what you got to say?" asked the planter.

"I say you're buyin' a dead man," answered Esau.

"Banjo-lips as alive as you and me," snapped the trader.

"I wouldn't buy him," said Esau.

"Why not?" asked the planter.

Esau walked over to the slave in question, stuck his thumbs into either side of the man's mouth, and pushed up his lips to expose the gums.

"Take your damn hands off my property," ordered the trader.

Esau ignored him.

"Lookit the man's gums," Esau said to the planter. "Got no color to 'em, and they's blisters, and they stink."

Indeed, the slave's gums were grayish white with suppurating blisters the size of black flies.

"Sambo's already rotten and ain't dead, yet," said Esau. "You won't get a month's work before you'll be planting him."

"Take 'em back," said the planter to the trader.

"I'll bring out another batch," said the trader.

"Not for me you won't," said the planter.

If looks could lay a man out flat. . .

"You killed my sale," said the trader.

"Just trying to help a neighbor out," replied Esau.

"You ain't no neighbor," spat the trader.

"So what?" said Esau challenging the man. "Sell your boys to somebody stupid."

"To hell with both of you," sputtered the trader, cracked his whip over the heads of his Negroes, and drove them back to the corral from which they came. The planter put his hand out to Esau and introduced himself.

"Cassius Tivitt, sir, and you are?"

"Esau Burdock."

"Mr. Burdock."

The two men shook hands.

"You're an impressive man, Mr. Burdock. England, right? What brings you to Natchez?"

"Business, Mr. Tivitt," answered Burdock.

"The slave trade?" asked Tivitt.

"It has been an area of interest. I represent a group of wealthy speculators in London. They're primarily interested in land, but I'm to keep my eyes out for good investments in whatever new world markets are available," answered Burdock.

"How do you come to know Negroes so well?"

"My business includes commodities, Mr. Tivitt. It's my job, sir, to know good from bad," said Burdock. *Be careful,* Esau said to himself. *This man Tivitt's got his eye on you. Just what do you think you're doing?*

Esau really did not know what he was doing, but he went ahead and did it, anyway. What he did know was that at this moment he was no longer an indentured servant but a man of the world, a gentleman of wealth and power. Tivitt saw him as an equal. It was a perception Esau relished enough to take his chances. Where would it lead?

Esau had learned plenty at *Hexley, Harlow & Hunt*, both from his masters as well as his masters' clientele: the rich, the haughty, those who had a secure place in this world (if anyone did). He could speak of sugar and cotton like a planter, French wine like an importer, burgeoning tobacco plantations of the upper South like a man with an interest in the future. He could speak of London and the search for foreign markets as the native he was. He knew the streets of fancy offices as well as the private clubs where business was done. However, there was an edge to him, and he knew that, too, an edge spoken to by the .75 caliber pistol clipped to his belt.

"You ever use that?" Tivitt wanted to know. Esau kept quiet. "Not exactly a dueling pistol, sir. May I?" asked Tivitt extending his hand. He examined the pistol like a watchmaker would a watch. "Did you get it this way?"

"Which way is that?" asked Burdock.

"Pistol like this used to be a flintlock. Somebody converted it to percussion. Was that your idea?" asked Tivitt.

"An uncle on my father's side was an officer in the British navy. The conversion was done by the admiralty's armorer. My uncle gave it to me on his deathbed."

"Heavy enough to use as a club."

"After it's fired. Yes, sir," said Esau.

"Put a hole in a man the size of a bucket," offered Tivitt.

"It will do that," said Esau, extending his hand to take it back. He clipped the pistol to his belt on the left side, easily reachable with his right hand, and covered it with his jacket. Still, any man could tell it was there with hardly a second look.

Esau knew enough about human nature to know that if you asked the right questions and kept a man talking about himself, kept a man expressing his opinions and giving you his advice, well, that man would think you the most interesting fellow walking in the world today. Tivitt became most animated when he talked of Natchez being the gateway to the West.

"May I call you Esau, young man?"

"Of course," Esau replied.

"If I were a young man on the move today I'd look to the West for my stake. New Mexico territory: there's the place. Ain't nothin' right now but godless savages, free land, and herds of wild horses. The only rules are the ones you make.

New Mexico, son. You heard it here first. You tell those folks back in London: New Mexico. Esau, that's the place you want to be. Say, you got plans for dinner?"

"I thought I'd take it at the inn," answered Esau.

"You stayin' there?"

"Not much to choose from. I'm planning to go back to New Orleans tomorrow."

"I got a little place up to Bayou Pierre you might like to see. Have dinner with us and spend the night," said Tivitt.

"I don't want to put anybody out," said Esau, hoping Tivitt would say nonsense and tell him come on.

"My house; my rules. You won't be putting anybody out," exclaimed Tivitt. "Get your horse and follow my carriage."

"Buying a horse was going be the next thing on my agenda. Mine died under me a few miles back," said Esau.

"Well, son, consider this your lucky day. I can fix you up with a horse won't die on you, feed you dinner, and put you in a bed so soft you'd believe you was on a cloud in Heaven. Come on. Ride with me," said Tivitt, who took Esau's arm and led him to his carriage. "They call this rig a barouche. Sounds like Hebrew talk, don't it? Barouche barouche, barouche." He slapped his knee and doubled up laughing.

———— ∞∞ ————

Cassius Tivitt's "little place" up to Bayou Pierre was a vast and self-sufficient plantation worked by a multitude of slaves, perhaps one thousand when you figured in not only the field hands but the blacksmith, shoemaker, farrier, gardeners, midwives, and all the other Negroes that had been taught a trade, plus the house servants: maids, butlers, cooks, and nannies. If you never left the place you'd still have pretty much whatever you needed. Cotton was the primary crop—thousands of acres—but Bayou Pierre also maintained a dairy herd, a beef herd, swine, and chickens, plus vegetable gardens and fruit trees.

"You won't go home hungry," promised Tivitt. "Let's get you on a horse first."

He directed the driver of the carriage to take a well-maintained dirt road that ran by the house and into the distant fields beyond. Esau had never seen such a spread, and it stoked his dreams. He'd barely heard of New Mexico either, but the things he learned from Tivitt seeped into his imagination and spread throughout his system like warm tea and whiskey. Godless savages? Well, Esau was godless himself, so that didn't bother him, and he could be savage, too. He'd fit right in. This made him laugh.

"What's funny?" Tivitt wanted to know.

"Just thinking," answered Esau.

"Man's got a joke he oughtn't to keep it to himself. The world could use a good laugh. Tell me," said Tivitt.

"I was thinking how proud my dear old mum would be of her baby boy if I had a spread like you, say in New Mexico. I'd build her a house next to mine and bring her over," replied Esau.

"Live out her years in a new world. Seein' her son be king of the castle."

"Just what I was thinking," said Esau.

"I think of all those wild horses running free. Nothing more beautiful. If I have another life I want to be running with them, right there at the front of the herd. Me. Cassius Tivitt. A white stallion with a valley full of brood mares. Nothing and nobody to challenge him. I doubt there's anything more beautiful in this world than a white stallion running flat out. Hell, even an ugly horse is beautiful running flat out, if there is such a thing as an ugly horse, which there ain't. Genghis Khan and those Mongol fellas practically lived on their horses. Their women cooked and carried, but nothing was more important to a warrior than his horse, and them boys was deadly with a bow and arrow. What they used to do was gallop into battle at full speed and wait 'til all four legs of the horse were off the ground before they fired an arrow. Gave 'em a steady aim."

Esau didn't know who Genghis Khan was, but he got the picture and liked it a lot.

"Yessir, them boys could ride," continued Tivitt. "From what I hear some of them red Indians must've got Mongol blood in 'em somewhere, way they ride. They got these little tiny horses—I swear ain't no bigger'n a pony but don't you call 'em that. They'll cut you down quick—got real short legs but, my God, they turn quick as a rabbit, shift direction so many times you think they're comin' one way and then they come at you another, firing arrows all the time. Don't you be thinking I desire to be some kind of Mongol, Mr. Burdock, but they can ride. I'll give 'em that. Country's movin' West and them Indians ain't gonna like it. Our army'd do good to breed a horse to match 'em. Pull up here, Amos," Tivitt said to his driver.

They stopped beside a large pasture fenced in by whitewashed pickets. Inside the pasture were maybe a dozen horses bred large, beautiful beasts, sleek but begot for power, coats ashine with the setting sun. Most were dark, some chestnut with sable markings, two buckskins with black manes and black tails, one gray, and one that seemed black until it moved, and then a darkish red tint, like a saddle of fire, became visible, revealing it to be a blood bay. Amos, the coachman, helped Tivitt climb down from the carriage. Burdock followed and joined the older man at the fence.

"Big man needs a big horse," said Tivitt. "You know Negroes, sir, but I know horses, and one of them is yours."

Esau remembered dray horses back in London that were big, but not as big, and nowhere near as beautiful. You looked at Tivitt's horses and right off saw one thing: power. Power. Even before you saw their beauty you saw their strength, brawny and robust, an unbeatable power that made their beauty even more astonishing. Tivitt went on.

"Horses like these were bred to carry knights in full armor, plus a steel skirt and mask for themselves. I breed 'em for myself. These won't ever pull a plow or a wagon. I just like to come out here and look at 'em, think of a time they terrorized the battlefield. Then the Mongols bred horses moved like acrobats, and their time went past. But nothing short of an elephant had the power they did, and I don't want to breed elephants nor camels nor rhinoceros. Graceless and ugly. What could be more beautiful than what I got right here?"

"And I get to choose one?" asked Esau, hoping he had the money in his pocket.

"It'd be my privilege to choose one for you, son," said Tivitt, informing Esau, basically, that the choice would not be his. "You did me a good turn back there at the market, and I want to give you back in kind. Each one out there takes a strong man to master them, but one's going to take a stronger man than the others. He's young, full of fire, and ready to test you at every step, but he's one of the gifts of God on this earth, and I believe you're the man to handle him. Are you that man, Mr. Burdock? Have you got the guts to ride her?"

"If the worst that can happen is I die trying, I'm your man," said Esau. And, in truth, he wasn't scared a bit. "Which one we talking about?" he asked.

"Which one you think?"

Esau stuck his little fingers into either side of his mouth and let out with a whistle so loud it could have come from a steamship. Every horse in the pasture raised their heads and looked to see where the sound had come from. Every horse in the pasture ambled slowly towards the men standing at the fence, all except one that bucked and kicked and headed in the opposite direction: the blood bay. Esau knew it was his.

"Call him Thor, Norse god of war. He had a red beard, and wherever he threw his hammer lightning struck," explained Tivitt. "Norse. First time I heard that word it reminded me of the snort of a giant battle stallion. That's Thor out there, son. If you can ride him he's yours."

Tivitt sent his driver to fetch tack, a bucket of oats, and a few pieces of molasses candy. He told him bring back Thomas and Old Sam, his most experienced stable hands, who worked with these horses and knew them like a mother knows her first born. The carriage returned shortly, and, when the two stable hands alighted, the entire herd, as if one, looked their way, and all but one walked deliberately towards the fence. All but one. Thor stayed where he was. The hands talked to the horses, called each by name and walked among them without fear, feeding each a handful of oats, scratching between their ears, running their hands firmly along the lengths of their massive necks.

"Give this man a couple pieces of candy, Thomas," said Tivitt.

Thomas took some of the molasses candy from his pocket and handed it to Esau.

"Up to you, Mr. Burdock," Tivitt said to Esau.

Suddenly, Esau wanted that horse worse than he ever wanted anything except his freedom. Red-bearded Thor, god of war, hammered lightning. His chariot pulled across the heavens by goats. Goats? Esau would go the god one better. One blood bay battle stallion. There was suddenly no doubt in his mind that he could do this.

"Gimme that," he ordered Old Sam, took the bit and bridle from him, and slung it over his shoulder so that the metal parts hung unseen behind him. He walked slowly towards the stallion, talking softly all the way. The stallion never took his eyes off the man, didn't sidle sideways, didn't seem in the least skittish and seemed, in fact, to be listening to what the man walking towards him had to say. Esau felt he had seen the horse in his dreams, and that the horse had seen him, too. They knew each other, didn't they? "It's you 'n' me, boy. Here we are like we was meant to be. Here we are, big fella. You 'n' me. Hear me, son. We're going to ride away, ride away, ride away. We're going to go far from here, far from here, you 'n' me. There's lots we haven't seen yet, lots we haven't seen yet, grain fields, rivers, trees with fruit we're bound to taste."

Esau stopped ten feet from Thor. The stallion had never moved his eyes from the man, watched with interest as Esau took a piece of candy from his pocket and held it out to him, held it out to him but stood still, stood where he was and waited for the stallion to come forward. The big horse laid back his ears, snorted and stomped, but kept his distance from the red-haired man ten feet in front of him. Esau clicked with his tongue against his teeth, varied the rhythm, sometimes fast, sometimes slow. The horse's ears came forward. He was listening, but he stood where he was and watched as Esau got down on all fours and inched forward. Once again the big horse snorted and stomped, only this time Esau tossed the piece of molasses candy at the stallion's feet. Thor reared back but caught the scent, lowered his massive head, and took the candy. Then he raised up and snickered for more. Esau rose slowly to his feet, took another piece of candy from his pocket, and held out his hand. Once again, the big horse snickered and stretched out his neck for more.

"Aw, no, son, this time you take it from the big man," said Esau in a soothing voice. "Take it from the big man. Take it from the big man. Take it from the big man," he whispered as he walked slowly forward, holding the candy so the stallion could see it. Thor snickered again, though this time Burdock saw it as a sign of pleasure, of desire, and continued forward. He stopped an arm's length away. The horse snaked out his head and tried to bite Esau, but the big man slipped gracefully aside like a prize fighter and smacked the horse on the side of his snout with everything he had. Thor shook his head and reared, but Esau bobbed under him and smacked him again. The man was fearless and stayed where he was, stayed in front of the horse with the molasses candy held out in the palm of his hand. They held each other's eyes. Thor shook his head vigorously side to side. Esau stayed where he was, the candy still held out in the palm of his hand. Thor watched as Esau took a bite of the candy himself. The sweetness of it filled his mouth with pleasure.

"You're missing some good stuff, amigo. Want some?" asked Esau.

Thor snickered and shook his head.

"Sure you do," crooned Esau. "Sure you do."

Thor snickered again; however, this time he lowered his head, sniffed, and took the candy with a slurp so loud the men back at the fence heard it and laughed. Thor then nuzzled Esau's pocket looking for more. Esau took another piece out and let the big horse take it from his hand once again, but this time, as the horse concentrated on the candy, Esau gently put the reins around his neck, clutched them lightly beneath the animal's throat, and walked him towards the fence.

"As fine a performance as I've ever seen," said Tivitt.

"Much obliged," said Esau smiling.

"Now you got to ride him. You don't need me to tell you it's a long way to the ground."

"Saddle him up, boys," ordered Esau as he scratched between Thor's ears and stroked his neck, talking to him all the while as the stable hands did what they were told.

"Old Sam's rode him," said Tivitt, "So's Thomas. Thor gave them a hard time but they're still with us. Ain't that right, boys?"

"We still here, yes, suh," replied Sam with a smile on his face.

"He liked to kill me," Tom chimed in. "Took me 'n Sam some before we settled him down."

"You don't want to be outrode by a couple of darkies, do you, boy?" Tivit asked Esau.

The taunt wasn't lost on Esau, not that it was so hard to grasp. The derision in Tivitt's voice was right out there for all to hear. He noticed Thor filled his belly with air while Old Sam tightened the cinch. Esau nudged Sam out of the way and launched a solid right into the big horse's midriff. Thor immediately let out his air, and Esau finished cinching him.

"You can feed him and cinch him. Now, let's see can you ride him," challenged Tivitt.

"Hold onto that 'til I say so," Esau ordered, and made certain Sam had the lead rope. Now Esau was a very big man, still he had to bring his left knee clear up to his chest so he could get his foot in the stirrup. He took the pommel in his left hand and swung his right leg up and over, settled into the saddle, and told Sam to let the stirrups down some. The ground was a long way away. The last time Esau was up this high was when he patched a piece of roof. Esau thought to himself, "Burdock, you've got three choices: You can make a damn fool of yourself, die, or ride this thing, and the first two ain't nowhere in the cards."

"Where do we send the body, son?" laughed Tivitt.

"Send it to Hell, Tivitt," snapped Esau. "I'll see you there."

Again, Tivitt just laughed. "Better take this," he said, and handed Esau a riding crop. "Keep the devil in his place." Esau put the crop between his teeth, shifted his weight in the saddle, took the reins lightly in his hands, said to Sam, "Let go the lead, boy," and touched his heels to the horse's flanks. Thor backed gently away from the fence until he was clear of the other horses. He didn't resist until Esau touched the reins to turn him out, at which point the animal yanked his head in the opposite direction and tried to turn back to the fence. "The hell you will," bellowed Esau and slammed his sledge hammer fist down between Thor's ears. The big horse felt it, shook his head, and tried to sit back on his haunches. Esau smacked its butt with the riding crop, and Thor shot forward like he'd been bit. Esau was astounded by the power of the beast beneath him, but shoved that thought from his mind because he had to ride, and if he dwelled on it he'd likely not.

Thor propelled himself into a full gallop, but Esau stayed with him and found it easier than tolerating the big horse's trot, a gait Esau wasn't that comfortable with, anyway. He rarely got the timing right—all that bumping up and down—and was always afraid he'd crush his family jewels between the saddle and his grandiose arse. However, at the gallop it was a smooth ride. The air rushing by Esau's face was flush with scent— magnolia blossoms, sweet timothy, clover, and fresh running water—so unlike the fetid atmosphere found at the slave market back in New Orleans. It came to him that he'd never felt so free before, had never felt free at all, in fact. But here he was, being treated as a gentleman, sitting a gentleman's horse, about to make a gentleman's transaction. If those back in London could see him now! His mother would gape, her rheumy eyes wide and yellow, the toothless hole in her face twisted into a smile, but that was an image he pushed out of his mind. He had come far, he had—recognized by Cassius Tivitt, a man of station and means, who gave Esau his due as an equal. Esau had never wanted anything more than he now wanted this horse. Price was a matter yet to be discussed. He truly hoped he had the money in his pocket to pay for it.

Esau was so intoxicated with the ride that he felt transported into another world, one where the thunder of hooves was like a heartbeat, and the rush of his blood was like a river carrying him towards enchanted territory. There would be tureens of fine food and bladders of wine like magic potions, beautiful women and spirited horses, herds of them coursing unrestrained across an endless plain, his endless plain, his. At first he could not hear the men calling him, hollering and yelling–what he did not know, but the sounds they made alarmed him. He'd gotten so carried away that he failed to notice Thor heading for a thick, old oak tree at the far end of the pasture. In that instant he realized the horse meant to brush him off against the tree. Esau pulled back on the reins but Thor plunged ahead anyway, fixed on the trunk of that tree. Esau thought, "This horse will not beat me. He will not beat me. He will not!" He reached down to his left, grabbed the rein near Thor's mouth, pulled it so that the horse was forced to turn in that direction, and then he slowed it down to a walk and kept him there as he returned to the fence where the men stood watching. The power. The power! He felt like Charlemagne, commander of paladins, master of his soul.

Tivitt shook his head in wonder. "Son, you had us chiseling your name on a tombstone," he said. "I thought you were gonna get grafted to that tree."

Old Sam attached Thor to a lead rope. Esau swung his leg over and jumped to the ground. His legs were so stretched out he felt as if he'd been tortured on the rack, or wild Indians had tied him to horses and ripped him apart at the crotch. Esau had to muster all his will to keep from walking like a drunk.

"How much?" he asked.

"I don't think we should discuss currency 'til after dinner," replied Tivitt.

"How much?" Esau insisted. "I'll eat better knowing he's mine. How much?"

Tivitt told him. Esau counted out the money from his pocket, and the two men shook hands on the deal.

"You got yourself a beauty," said Tivitt.

Esau knew it.

Delphine Eustacia Simone de Fleur Tivitt, called Ol' Miss by her husband, Cassius Tivitt, master of Bayou Pierre, ruled as the lady of the manor. She was born into a family of wealthy aristocrats three generations removed from France. But by the time Delphine came of age, mismanagement and profligacy had reduced the de Fleurs to the status of land poor. Delphine's parents sold the last of their vast holdings at a good price to Cassius Tivitt, a shrewd merchant well below their station, with the stipulation that he would marry Delphine, their oldest daughter. She had been a plump child with a fierce temper who tyrannized her family for not supplying her every whim as their fortune drained away. They were glad to be rid of her, especially since it meant that with Tivitt's money they could retire gracefully to a house that befit them in the city of Natchez. By the time the Tivitts were in the third year of their marriage, they despised each other. Delphine's parents did her a favor by dying in a shipwreck on their return from a visit to the family's ancestral acreage in France. They left the house in Natchez to her, albeit with the burden of unpaid taxes. Tivitt was tempted to let the house go at auction, but Delphine pleaded with him to keep it, which he did on the proviso that the property be put into his name. She dearly wanted that house as an escape from plantation life, where she could entertain her lady friends, play cards, and generally indulge life in the city. Tivitt's fervent wish was that she use it more often.

Burdock and Tivitt were met at the entrance to the big house by a regal servant dressed in a well-tailored black suit, white shirt, and gray silk tie. He was a dark-skinned Negro, tall and well proportioned, with a hide almost as shiny as the shoes on his feet, and it crossed Burdock's mind that the man might be a kind of bodyguard, Tivitt's first line of defense at the front door.

"Hullo, Ulysses, where's the mistress?" asked Tivitt. A woman's voice was heard screaming from upstairs. "Never mind," said Tivitt.

"Get away from me, Livy, you idiot," the woman yelled. A young girl, a beautiful child of fifteen or so, ran in a near panic down the curving staircase, tripped, fell, and disappeared into another room. She was light-skinned with blonde hair, so much so she seemed white, though Esau recognized in the instant that she was not. She had a slight broadening of the nose, a subtle fullness of the lips. Someone else might not notice, but Esau knew an octoroon when he saw one, a "high-yella fancy" she'd be called at the market. Tivitt would have the envy of any man who saw her, though his stated reason for purchase was to give his wife more help in the kitchen, maybe help with the sewing, too. But, really, the girl was his, no secret to anyone.

"Ol' Miss must be beating her again," offered Tivitt, "It's a damn nuisance the way she's always hitting the girl. I got a bargain on her 'cause she's prone to running away. I told her she'd never get a whipping from me for running away. What I'll do, I told her, is turn the dogs out on her. Shred the bitch in seconds, and she knows I mean it."

Delphine appeared at the top of the stairs red faced, apoplectic with anger. Esau thought he'd never seen an uglier woman in his life, unless it was his mother.

"I want her beaten, Mr. Tivitt. I tell you, sir, I want her beaten," she bellowed. "Bloodied and in the quarters with the rest of the baboons where she belongs."

"What's she done wrong now?" asked Tivitt.

"More like what's she done right, sir!"

"Maybe if you didn't rant on her so much she'd get the hang of things," replied Tivitt.

"You dare defend her and not me?" shrieked Mrs. Tivitt. "How dare you, sir! You and whoever that is with you can get your own damn dinner. All the hell you like is jungle food, anyway," she hollered, turned like she was an actress on a stage, and disappeared from the landing. Tivitt seemed barely ruffled by his wife's performance. "Don't worry, Mr. Burdock. Livy will serve us. I won't be getting indigestion, either," said Tivitt.

Dinner was, as Cassius Tivitt promised, a delicious and relaxing affair: roast pork, yams, black-eyed peas, mustard greens, corn bread, fresh milk, and honey custard for dessert. Livy dropped nothing and made no mistakes that Esau could see, though it was apparent she kept herself out of Tivitt's reach whenever possible.

"Show this gentleman what you got, Livy," he said at one point, and made her stand and turn to show herself off to Esau. She was a beauty, and Esau could tell why a man might desire her. Certainly, Tivitt did. She made Esau catch his own breath, too. After dinner, he took Esau into the library for brandy and cigars.

The brandy (actually, an Armagnac) was imported. Tivitt made certain to bring Esau's attention to the way the Armagnac sheeted the glass. Esau tucked that fact into his memory: Finer people drank Armagnac.

The two men sat side by side in imposing leather armchairs. Between the two chairs stood a small walnut table on graceful legs that seemed too dainty for it. A highly polished box carved from tropical cocobolo wood and fitted with small brass hinges rested on the table. It would not have surprised

Esau if Tivitt had opened the chest and scooped out a fist full of gold coins. However, inside that box was treasure of another kind. He held the box under Esau's nose and opened it.

"Rolled on the thighs of Cuban virgins, my friend," said Tivitt with a leer, as both men feasted on the aroma of fine, fresh, pungent tobacco. Cuban cigars. Big around as a man's thumb. This was nothing like that wretched herb Esau got from the Choctaws. The box opened and a genie was set loose, an aroma that overwhelmed the senses and made the two men drunk with pleasure. This was why God in His celestial glory created tobacco.

"Have a cigar," said Tivitt. Esau took one, and Tivitt did the same for himself. "Ain't got nothin' like this in England do they, son?" Esau almost said he didn't know, he hadn't been there for a long time, but he caught himself and said, "No, sir."

"Spain makes 'em, but they ain't nearly this good," Tivitt said as he bit off the end and spit it into the brass spittoon at his feet. "Bet you can't do that, young man," challenged Tivitt.

"No, sir," said Esau, biting off the end of his cigar, as well.

"I can still hit what I spit at. May the good Lord keep me in my senses," said Tivitt, almost wistfully, almost as if he meant it. He busied himself getting a spark from his tinderbox, a modern version that sported a flint wheel, then used it to light the tip of a splint that had been dipped in sulfur. With that he lit his cigar, turning it slowly to get an even burn before passing the burning splint to Esau.

"One of these days somebody's gonna make this thing can light itself, somebody out there tinkering on it right now. If I could find him I'd put smart money on him quick."

The heavy walnut doors to the library opened and slammed back against the wall, propelled by the energy of Tivitt's seven-year-old granddaughter, Daphne Aphrodite. "Grandpa, grandpa, grandpa," she squealed as she launched herself onto

his lap, all blonde ringlets, smoochy kisses, and porcelain perfect skin. Tivitt hugged her and dandled her, called her "my
little treasure" and was absolutely captivated by the child.
Daphne Aphrodite was staying with her grandparents while her
mother and father were in New Orleans on business. Her
nanny, Teeny May, a plump, white-haired, dark brown woman,
a family servant for generations, bustled in behind her.

"You got a 'pointment with a bar of soap, Miss Daphne,"
she said.

"Give an old man five more minutes, will you, Teeny
May?" asked Tivitt. "Yes, sir," she said.

"You stand right there, Teeny May, while I read grandpa
my poem," said Daphne Aphrodite.

"Yes, ma'am," answered Teeny, who smiled and stood
back.

"Did you read grandpa your poem, yet?" asked Ol' Miss as
she, too, entered the room. "Wait'll you hear this, Mr. Tivitt,"
she said, "I believe we've got a little Calliope on our hands.
The muse of epic poetry and eloquence, Mr. Burdock. She
even wrote it down! Go on, Daphne. Read it to us." Ol' Miss
was so proud. "Have you heard it, yet, Teeny?"

"Oh, yes, ma'am, Miss Daphne she read it to me while she
was writin' it," she said with a big smile.

"You won't mind, will you, Mr. Burdock?" inquired Ol'
Miss.

"Not a bit," said Esau.

Daphne Aphrodite climbed down from her grandfather's
lap and, clearing her little throat, promptly commanded abso-
lute attention from the center of the room. She took a piece of
paper from her bodice and unfolded it with great ceremony.
"Ahem." She looked around to make certain she had everyone's attention, and when she was sure she had, she launched
into her performance.

"I wish I had a thousand slaves or more
To catch the raindrops as they pour
I'd dress them in silver and satin and gold
And they will still love me when I'm very old."
The end.

In truth, Esau would just as soon have smacked the child, cut off her hair, and sold it to the gypsies, but he smiled and clapped with everyone else.

"Was I good, Teeny?" asked the child.

"Oh, yes, Miss Daphne. Calliope. Like your grandma say," answered Teeny May.

"Now," said Ol' Miss, "Time for our bath and hot milk, young lady. Teeny, see that she drinks her milk while she's still in the tub."

"Hear that, miss?," asked Teeny May.

"Good night, Grandpa," Daphne called, and blew him a dramatic kiss. Then she turned and skipped across the floor. "Come on, Teeny," she said.

"Yes, ma'am," answered Teeny May, and the two of them headed out the door, Daphne Aphrodite first. She ran smack into Livy as the slave girl walked through the door carrying a silver tray and coffee service. To Livy's horror, everything she carried crashed to the floor.

"My God, girl, what have you done?" yelled Ol' Miss, and smacked Livy across the face. "Get down there and clean that up this instant!" Livy dropped to her knees and began cleaning up the mess. "You dented the coffee service, damn you," yelled Ol' Miss, and she kicked Livy in the side. Daphne Aphrodite stepped around her and continued out the door.

"I want you to come upstairs and say goodnight to me, too, Livy," said the little girl. "Come on, Teeny."

"You didn't answer her, girl," said Ol' Miss.

"Yes, ma'am," said Livy.

"To her!"

"Yes, ma'am," Livy said to Daphne Aphrodite, who by now was gone and paying no attention whatsoever.

"I brook no insolence in this house, you little bitch," said Ol' Miss, as she unbuckled a leather belt from around her waist.

"No, ma'am, please," Livy pleaded, but no amount of appeal kept her from a beating. Two, three, five times across the back with the belt. The girl took it on her hands and knees. As the old woman raised her arm for number six, Tivitt called out, "That's enough, Missus." But, Ol' Miss hit the girl again even harder than before. "I said stop it, Mrs. Tivitt."

"Get out of here," she yelled at the girl. Livy got to her feet with the ruined service.

"What do you say?" demanded Ol' Miss.

"Yes, ma'am."

"I'm sorry, ma'am," demanded her mistress.

"I'm sorry, ma'am," Livy said and hurried away.

"How dare you call me down in front of a slave girl," spat the old woman at her husband. "I want her out of here, Mr. Tivitt. Take her back where you got her." She grabbed her skirts and rushed from the room in a fury.

"Eve sure as hell messed it up for the rest of us poor pilgrims," moaned Tivitt. "I think my wife's beat that poor child every day since she got here. I bought the girl to help Ol' Miss with the kitchen and sewing and whatnot, but she turned out to be quite versatile, if you know what I mean," he said, with a wink and a tip of his snifter. "Breaks my heart, but I'm gonna have to sell her. I don't, I got war on my hands."

The library doors opened and Livy walked in carrying a new service for coffee.

She stood straight and fought to keep her tears for herself.

"Here I get a breath of fresh air, and my wife wants to stop me breathin'," grumbled Tivitt. "You married, Mr. Burdock?"

"Ain't had the pleasure, sir," answered Esau.

"Get married and you won't have the pleasure, either, son," quipped Tivitt. "Put that down right here, Livy," He patted the walnut table beside him. She'd been standing there waiting. Burdock thought this one was a beauty: silky yellow hair with skin like honey. Closest to white you'd ever get. A fancy. Any man who had one was envied by every man who didn't.

"The fountain of youth lies between those legs. Just lookin' at her gimme another ten years of life," said Tivitt. He lifted the hem of her dress with his walking stick. "Her privy parts is yella, too." The girl stood still and stared out somewhere over their heads. "Imagine what her young will fetch if you breed her right. Money in the bank."

"I'll give you a thousand for her," said Esau. Tivitt removed his walking stick from the hem of Livy's dress and let the frock fall again to its full length. He leaned on his walking stick and focused on Esau.

"You'll gimme two," retorted Tivitt.

"The girl still needs to be broken," answered Esau, "She's got scars, and your missus don't want her."

"You're gonna skin me on this one, ain't you, Mr. Burdock?"

"A thousand's fair market," said Esau.

"To lose this child and get skinned in the bargain, son, you're puttin' a wagon load of sorrow on an old man's heart, but the truth is, I got to get her out of here before the missus kills her. Tell you what, throw in a case of French brandy and we'll close," offered Tivitt. "It'll dull the pain."

———— ❦ ————

When Livy approached her womanhood, long before she found herself bought by Cassius Tivitt, the older women on the plantation where she lived, knowing what was ahead for her, took her into their confidence and taught her what they knew about having babies and, more importantly, about not having babies. The women had all kinds of advice depending upon where in Africa they had come from, or what other women had told them when they were young, because a slave girl who looked like Livy could never get too much information. She was her master's whim and had to protect herself as best she could. One thing she was told was to plug her vagina with a mixture of sweet gum, honey, and acacia leaves. However, since there were no acacia trees in the United States, you'd grind up Queen Anne's lace and work it through the mixture. There were other suggestions, too. Dislodge the sperm by jumping backwards seven times. Take a small plug of wool and soak it in a mixture of tobacco juice, ginger, and lemon. Stick a copper penny in there. Sit over a pot of hot stewed onions. Stick in a plug of wood anointed with honey, cedar, resin, and juice of the balsam tree. Douche with vinegar. But, the best way, if you could, was to fool the master by making him think he was inside you when he was not. "When he go to stick it in you take him tight 'tween both thighs, make him believe he be right where he want to be. He won't know nothin' different."

———— ∞∞ ————

When Esau awoke at Bayou Pierre in the morning he found the girl sleeping on the floor at the foot of his bed. A few hours later, after breakfast, she rode behind him on the blood bay stallion as they headed south to New Orleans. Esau Burdock was the proudest man in Mississippi.

———— ∞∞ ————

Reuben Moon
Mescalero Territory
November 17, 1817

REUBEN FOUND THE WOMAN SQUATTING IN A THICKET OF cottonwood trees beside a slender tributary of a rushing creek. She maintained her balance by holding onto a branch above her head, and she bit down hard on a stick in her mouth to stifle her cries, for she was in terrible pain. The moans that escaped her were muffled by the flowing water, though Reuben, whose hearing was as keen as a deer's, heard enough to guide him to her in the dark. Because the sky was on fire, he could see enough to know that this one had escaped her master. He'd seen her before when she came to the settlement of New Hope, tagging along behind her master and watched over by a bossy African whose sole job it seemed was not to let her charge out of sight. Now here she was, alone, that same girl, young, pregnant, and trying to birth her baby. The girl was light-skinned with hair the color of wine matted around her face from sweat. The instant she saw him she tried to get to her feet and run, but she had little strength left, fell to the ground, and did what she could to crawl. Her fingers dug into the loamy soil as she tried to drag herself away from the man she thought was there to take her back. He knelt beside her, held her head, and eased her onto her back saying, "Hush now. I won't hurt you. I'm here. I'll help." The girl tried to hit him, but was so weak her blows were merely pats.

"Don' take me back," she begged, "Don' take me back!"

"No, no," Reuben said softly, held her head and tried to calm her. "Tell me your name." She wrenched her head away—"Lemme be! Lemme be!—but he held her and looked into her eyes, and she knew that he would not harm her. "Lilly Rose. My baby," she said.

Reuben could see how swollen her belly was, how narrow were her hips. The infant could not come out no matter how hard the girl pushed. She struggled to take a gold chain bearing a carved green stone from around her neck, but she couldn't do it. He took the gold chain in his hands, the green stone carved like some kind of pot-bellied smiling god he'd seen Indians do.

"Please," she said. He took the gold chain from around her neck. "My mother's," she said. "My baby's. Please," she said again, and then she died with her eyes wide and staring at some terrible sight only she could see.

Reuben closed her eyes and gently lowered her head to the ground. He laid his hands upon her and could feel no movement. He lifted her dress and saw that the baby's head had tried to push its way out, but it looked as big as a melon, and Reuben knew that birth this way was impossible, if it weren't already dead. He took his knife and searched her belly, seeking the best place to cut. The woman's stomach was so grossly swollen that Reuben feared the point of his knife would burst her apart and toss her guts, maybe her infant, high into the branches of the surrounding trees. He had to go slowly, shallow slices one at a time as he worked his way through to where her womb held the infant. He made his first cut and his second and his third until the stomach gaped wide open before him. Reuben could see the infant now, partially hidden by tissue and the remnants of its sac. It was on its back, a girl child. Her little belly spasmed as she struggled for breath. Reuben cut the cord and gently lifted her free. Her tiny hands clenched and unclenched; her little legs kicked out. She struggled. He put his index finger in her mouth to make sure she was clear and that her tongue was in the right place. Still, she struggled. He took her nose in his mouth and sucked as hard as he could, sucked out the scum that was blocking her and spit it out. He blew into her mouth until he felt her stomach expand, blew some more until it moved in and out on its own, regular and even, and the next instant she screamed so shrilly Reuben half expected a shriek back. Her lungs were clear. She screamed long and loud. She would not be denied her place. This little thing. Not so little, really, but long for a new-born with hair nearly white. Was this infant born wise, he wondered? How did the mother come to bear this baby in the wilderness, far from hot water and a bed and women to tend her? The mother had come a long, hard way, but her baby was here now, and why ever she was she would die if he didn't attend to her. He removed the shawl worn by her mother, wrapped the infant in it, laid her carefully on the ground, and adjusted her feet so they wouldn't hang out and get cold. Then he tore open the top of the woman's dress and exposed her breasts, large and full, nipples the deep purple of ripe figs . . . or bruises. The baby girl screamed even louder. She didn't sound sad or scared; she sounded angry. She was insisting she be given what she wanted. Reuben thought, what a creature! She would not be denied, demanded her due, let you know she was there, and he thought, "Can you like a baby? Do I like this thing? Quiet. Be quiet. I will take care of you."

Reuben picked her up and cradled her, placed her needy mouth upon her mother's nipple, held her there, and watched the child paw at the breast and suck with a ferocity born of soul, not just hunger.

———— ∞∞∞ ————

The storm from Trapper Peak had eased off to a chilly mist that enveloped Reuben Moon as he passed through Wild Horse Canyon and rode out upon a wide plateau. The Mescalero encampment stood far away, at the plateau's eastern end—the confluence of two rivers. You could see where the waters met because one was red and the other dark brown. The new sun rose behind the village. Whorls of smoke, stirred by a morning breeze, floated upward from the village huts, wikiups made of wattle and branches, teepees interspersed. The infant, covered over with the buffalo robe, slept with her head against Reuben's bare chest. He felt her drool on his skin. He knew where she had come from; he knew he would never take her back. There was a woman who lived on the outskirts of the village. He would place a stone and a feather at the entrance to her hut. Reuben would offer her the child. He would promise her food and warm robes for as long as he lived, and he would see.

Reuben never forgot that he had himself been an orphan, a slave raised in an enemy camp. While he lived with the Comanche, a day did not go by when he thought of the humiliation inflicted upon him. Boy, keep up with the wagon or get dragged on the ground! He kept up even as the sharp detritus of the trail bit into the bare soles of his feet. He kept up and brooded about the day—one day—when he would ram a lance through the chest of his father's murderer. But when he was sixteen, a fever raged through the tribe and robbed Reuben of his revenge by reducing the old warrior to a cinder of himself, and stealing his mind so that he recognized no one when he died. The tribe mourned his death and so did Reuben, but for different reasons. That same day Reuben took his horse from the herd and rode south towards New Mexico, where he had been born. Whatever part of him had become Comanche he left behind.

───────◦◦◦◦◦◦◦───────

The woman without a nose returned to her wikiup with a day's load of firewood on her back. She wore a patch of deer hide held by thongs tied around her head to cover the scar where her nose had been crudely hacked off. Mostly, she avoided people, but on those rare occasions when she was forced to be with others she never went without it, rarely took it off even when alone inside her hut. Without it she might feel for a moment that she was whole. But that was a lie she told herself for an instant's peace, a single second when she might be beautiful again instead of the disfigured hag she had become. She set her shelter on the encampment's perimeter mostly hidden by a large oak. Unless a person came upon her she wouldn't be seen. She knew they called her ugly, ugly, ugly. It was her shame, and, more days than not, she wished for death. Many nights she lay on her robes with a knife held to her breast, though she hadn't yet found the nerve to roll over on it.

Reuben watched her at a distance from behind a dense thicket of chokecherry brush. The woman was without her nose patch. She saw the stone and eagle feather he had placed there while she was out gathering wood, saw it well before she reached the entrance to her hut, dropped the wood where she stood, and hurried to pick up the feather. She looked on both sides of it as if expecting to see a message, then looked around her to see who left it there. Her eyes lit on the chokecherries, passed them by, then snapped back. It was the logical place to hide. With a cry she stooped and ran inside.

How careless, how stupid was she not to have worn her patch! She should have known better. Her name had been "Dear One" – *Pritta*. Now she was known as "Eyesore," "No Nose," "Gruesome," "Gristle." Her husband had cast her out. Her lover had disappeared. Children threw stones at her to keep her away. She was welcome at no one's fire. She had been reduced to two emotions: hatred for them and pity for *Pritta*, who was gone. She had become loathsome even to herself, but someone had left a message for her outside her doorway. An eagle feather on a rock meant something important. Who could want something from her? What? And why would they?

She took her patch from a twig that jutted out of the wall, placed it over where her nose had been, and tied the thongs behind her head. "Who wants me?" she shouted. She did not like the way her voice quavered, and shouted again, "Who wants me?" Better. *I am not afraid of them*, she thought. She heard footfalls approach her doorway. She heard the whimper of an infant. The wind. It must be the wind, a tree branch rubbing against another. It couldn't be the child she lost. God wouldn't be that cruel. Hadn't she been cursed enough?

"Reuben Moon," he answered. He'd never spoken a word to her before, as far as she knew had never so much as looked her way.

"Go away."

"It's important."

"Go away."

"Let me in."

"No."

There was that whimper again.

"Stop it," she said, refusing to believe it was what it was.

"She needs warmth, a roof, food. I brought her to you."

"A child?"

"She needs to eat. Turn around if you don't want me to see you."

"Oh, oh, oh. . ."

He pulled aside the hide that covered the doorway, stooped, and came through. He shrugged the buffalo robe from around his shoulders. She saw the shawl in his arms and watched as he moved the cloth away and showed her the baby's face, the pale skin, the hair nearly white.

"Oh, oh, oh," was all she could manage.

"Take her," he said. "There's no one else."

Reuben had tied an amulet around the baby's wrist to keep her safe from harm, a small piece of oak that had been struck by lightning. He'd also taken the necklace from her mother, shortened it by tying a knot in its gold chain, and put it around the baby's neck.

"Her mother?" asked the woman.

"Dead."

He held the baby out to her and now she took it.

"Oh, oh, oh." The perfect ears. Corn silk hair. The tiny mouth. Green eyes. Gem stones. The little nose. "Oh, my. Oh, my." She sat and crossed her legs, cradled the infant and took out her breast. It no longer mattered that Reuben was there. "Make us a fire," she said, placed her nipple in the baby's mouth, and squeezed in the first drop of milk. My God, the child could suck! She was rough, this child, and suddenly bit down hard. The woman flinched; her breast fell from the infant's mouth. The child let out a yelp and waved her little arms about. One little hand accidentally caught the thong that held the patch to the woman's face. The patch came down and exposed the scar, but the baby screamed for her breast and all the woman could think was to give it back to her. The child sucked but kept her eyes on the woman's face and did not turn away. The woman felt sure she smiled. As the infant's belly filled and swelled with milk, so, too, did the woman's heart with the infant. All the love she would have given to the child she lost was flowing to this new creature, and she knew then that she would love this child forever.

It was the Christians who later named her Sojourner.

The child was just beginning to walk when the spots first appeared. Soon her body was covered with small sores the size of ticks, and burning with fever. She tore at her clothes and screamed at the slightest touch of anyone's hand. Holy men lit fires around her wickiup, painted demons in the sand, and flushed them out with sacred water. But the fever continued to rage, until finally the holy men began to chant and sing the songs that would accompany the child to the world beyond. Reuben refused to accept this. There was said to be a doctor at a mission three days up river. The holy men begged him to keep the child in camp. They said at least she would have their prayers. Let them send a runner for the doctor. Once more Reuben refused. He knew there was no guarantee a stranger would come anywhere near the encampment. There were devils here, and even if the man did come, would he get there in time?

Her sores were beginning to fester. "Get me horses," he ordered. The child wailed when he touched her, terrible cries that pierced his heart, but Reuben did what was needed and attached her like a papoose to Pritta's back. Then he and the woman mounted up. He forbade the holy men to burn the wickiup until he was a day away. There were demons in it, and he did not want the lethal creatures to follow the three of them up river. The holy men lit a fire in front of the entrance to the wickiup and kept the encircling fires burning. Even as the three were lost to sight, the holy men sang and chanted until they could no longer hear the little girl's cries.

They followed the river. Except for watering the horses, their intent was not to stop until they reached the mission, a three day journey, in less than two. They ate jerky and slept on horseback. When Reuben slept, Pritta led and held onto his lead rope, and when she slept he did the same with hers. The sky was overcast so the moon was no help, but they kept the river on their right and picked their way forward. Pritta took the child from her back and rode with her cradled in her arms. When the child slept, which she did only in fits and starts, she gasped for breath; when she was awake she wailed and howled like a trapped little beast. At one point Reuben was certain he heard a cat cry back. But worst of all was when she was quiet, and then Pritta had to put her ear to the girl's nose to satisfy herself that the tiny thing still breathed.

They reached the mission the afternoon of the second day. It was a small cabin made of wood and well constructed, though not yet weathered, so Reuben knew its occupants had been in this country but two years at most. An outbuilding used as a workshop stood to one side. Its doors, wide as a small barn and open to let in the light, revealed a sawmill and a wood lathe. An immaculate garden that surprised Reuben by its size held winter squash not yet harvested, and the aroma of smoked meat wafted from a smokehouse that Reuben guessed was out back. A chill had set in, borne by a slight breeze. The child, who had been sleeping, moaned and stirred, so Pritta hugged her closer. A man, white but with a kind smile, laid down his tools and stopped his work on a large wooden chest, one suitable for linens, took off his leather carpenter's apron, stretched out his back, and stood up to greet them. He wore a wide-brimmed black hat, a black waistcoat over a linen shirt, and deerskin breeches. In place of boots he wore black shoes, each with a tarnished brass buckle.

"Welcome, friends," he said.

Pritta looked to Reuben to tell her what the man said. Reuben answered her in Apache.

"You speak English?" asked the man. Reuben nodded.

"Forgive my poor Apache," the man said, "I'm still learning it."

A white woman bustled out from behind the mission dressed in a plain brown dress, black cloak, and black silk bonnet with clogs on her feet. She and the man exchanged looks that Reuben guessed were some signal between them.

"Welcome, friends," she said, turning to them with a smile of her own.

Each wore a silver cross around their necks. Reuben did not believe the way they did, but he heard from others that there was magic to be gotten from it, and he hoped it would be more powerful than the magic of the holy men. Even with a beard the man looked young to him, though Reuben tossed that thought aside because he had gotten to the age where everyone looked young to him. If these people had the faith to thrive in the wilderness and swear allegiance to some trusted goodness, maybe they had the power to heal his little girl. That thought took Reuben by surprise. He had never thought of her as his before. The child had changed him. He would have to think about that but not now. Now she was in the white man's hands.

Pritta swung her right leg over her horse's neck and slid to the ground with the child still in her arms. The woman reached for the little girl, but Pritta refused to let her go.

"She's very sick," said Reuben.

"Yes, we can see that," said Joel, for that was his name. "Eden," he said to his wife, "Get a sheet and soak it in cold water. First thing we've got to get that fever down." Eden took a brass bucket from a hook on the porch and hurried to fill it from the creek that ran alongside the mission. To Pritta he said in butchered Apache, "Bring the child inside." She didn't understand him, so again she looked to Reuben. He nodded towards the door. Joel reached for the child, but Pritta would not give the child up and carried her inside herself.

The front room was a sitting room, uncluttered and plainly furnished with muslin curtains, two rocking chairs, and a simple bench along the back wall such as one might find in a simple church. It was beautifully crafted, as was the floor beneath it made with wide pine planks immaculately fit together. The room was clean and inviting. Reuben saw no weapons except an old trade gun, fair for hunting, that hung over the fireplace.

Joel led them into a side room that served as a doctor's office. An examining table sat in the middle, padded with a buffalo robe and covered with a spotless white sheet. It was as neat and clean as the other, though shelves on one wall held varied containers, glass and tin, of powders, ointments, dried herbs, lotions, and potions. Joel patted the table and indicated that Pritta should put the child down.

"Undress her, please," he said, the "please" and the pronoun both said in Apache. Pritta removed the child's wraps until she lay naked on the table. Joel did not express surprise either at the color of her hair or the fairness of her skin. He examined the lesions and found some on her scalp as well. "Whose child is this?" he wondered, but instead he asked, "What's her name?" Reuben translated for Pritta. She shrugged and answered, "The little one."

"You've come a long way, haven't you, young lady?" Joel said to the child. His voice was soft and gentle. She kept her eyes on his face and whimpered a bit, but didn't cry. Eden came in with a cool, damp sheet, still in the brass bucket though no longer wringing wet. She, too, took note of the little girl's fair features and wondered where she had come from, though, like her husband, she said nothing. These people had a way about them, so calm and caring, and they made Reuben feel calm, too. The same for Pritta, calm, still worried, but calm. And the little girl, more at peace than in many days.

Joel said something to Eden that Reuben didn't understand. The Indians watched as she took a tin of dried leaves from the medicine shelf that had been ground into a greenish powder. Another tin held an ointment. She scooped out some, placed it on a small plate, mixed it with the powder, and handed it to Joel. One by one he put the mixture over each of the little girl's sores.

"This will stop the itching and draw out the poison," he said.

He turned her on her stomach and covered the rest. When he had finished, Eden wrapped her in the cool white sheet.

"Hello there, young lady," she said, touched her finger to the tiny mouth, made a silly noise. Was that a little smile? Was it? "Come on now. Let's see you smile," coaxed Eden.

"I want the three of you to sleep here tonight. The little one shouldn't travel, not if we want her to be stronger by morning. We'll pile extra buffalo robes on the floor for you," said Joel in a voice that was as stern as he ever allowed himself to be. Reuben nodded and translated for Pritta, who again took the child in her arms. She could see that Reuben trusted these people, and so would she. When she moved to pick up the child, Joel placed his hand on the little girl and asked Pritta to wait.

"I have a prayer I'd like to say," he said, "And a name I'd like to use." Again, Reuben translated for Pritta. He knew this was more of the man's magic, trusted it would do no harm, hoped it would help. He nodded, yes.

Joel removed his cross, closed the child's fingers around it, and held her hand in his. He named his gods and said his prayer, took the cross and pressed it gently to the child's forehead then to her lips, put it back around his neck and said softly, "I should like to call you Sojourner." She actually smiled at him as he said it.

Reuben said, "Sojourner." He looked at Pritta and repeated, "Sojourner." Pritta said it, too, "Journey." She made it sound soft and sweet, like a songbird in a bower. *Jernee, Jernee* . . . and that is how the little girl came by her name.

For dinner that evening, Eden cooked a special soup she was taught to make by her grandmother, chicken with eggs and barley. She killed a fat hen, removed the ovaries, took the meat off the bones, and cooked it with barley and celery until it was nearly as thick as stew. She placed a platter of warm, fresh biscuits in the center of the table, and they drank the soup piping hot from bowls of cherry wood turned by Joel. Pritta held Journey in her lap and fed her with a wooden spoon, or she would soak a piece of biscuit in the broth and place them in the child's mouth. There was enough hot coffee for seconds and thirds, and raspberries with sweetened goat's milk for desert. By the end of dinner, they all were certain that Journey seemed stronger. There was still an hour of daylight left. Pritta took Journey into the examining room to sleep, while Eden cleaned from dinner. Joel and Reuben went outside to put up the stock for the night. The mules were fed, the pigs slopped, the goats milked, and the chickens in their coop when the two horsemen rode up from the direction of New Hope, still the nearest settlement to the east.

Joel went to greet them, but Reuben drew back and watched from the shadows. The men wore buckskins and moccasins, ponchos and red woolen hats like French trappers, and both were mounted on Indian ponies, smallish horses with scarred hides and spindly legs but tough, the type that could dart like grasshoppers and run all day. Each carried a flintlock musket in a saddle scabbard, large knives with elk horn handles at their waists, and coils of rope around their pommels. The larger and older of the two men had a packhorse behind him on a lead rope, and both men had two sets of chains and manacles slung over their saddles in front of them. They seemed the very opposite of goodness, a malevolence that made one want to keep one's distance. They had the stench of men who rarely bathed. The larger and older sported an unkempt array of facial hair braided at the chin and tied with a ribbon. He exuded the power of an ox.

The younger man, too skinny by half, but hard as barbed wire, stared like a cobra. He had an affliction whereby his skin took on the grayish pallor of white birch. His tongue and gums were the same, and his teeth were filed into points. Joel knew what they were. He had seen them before in New Hope leading a string of manacled Africans as they now led the packhorse. Reuben knew, too. These men were slave catchers. They hunted down escaped chattel and returned them for the reward.

"Heard a rumor that runaways stop here on their way to Mexico," said the older, dispensing with any preliminaries. "Harboring's a criminal act."

"Nonesuch here," said Joel

"You bein' a man of God like they say, you wouldn't want to do no wrong. Take a look around," said the older man to his partner. Without waiting to hear what Joel might have to say, without caring really, the skinny one touched his heels to his horse and walked him around the mission and its outbuildings.

"You there," he called to Reuben, "Come out where I can see ya." Reuben did, and the large man looked him over. "What're you doin' here?" he asked.

"His child took sick. He brought her to me," answered Joel.

"Can't you talk?" the man asked Reuben.

"He's my guest," said Joel.

"Don't mean he can't talk. You ain't afraid he's gonna steal you blind?" asked the slave catcher.

"That's for me to worry about, not you," snapped Joel.

"Bushpigs' 'n' skins friend. Got to be careful. You take care. She in the house?"

"Who?" asked Joel.

"Your woman."

"Yes."

"Who else?"

"The child and her mother."

"Go look," the older man told the skinny one who had come back from his look see.

"I told you the truth," Joel protested.

"Many's the time I swore to the truth when it wasn't so," the older one said. "Go look," he ordered the other.

The skinny one, who wasn't more than eighteen, dismounted and walked into the house. Eden came out to stand on the porch while he was in there.

"Joel?" she asked.

"It'll be fine," he said.

No one outside spoke another word while they waited for the skinny one to come back.

"Squaw and a kid," he said once he did. "Only Indians."

"Rumors bein' what they are," said the older one, "Who can tell? Stay here and entertain these people," he said to the skinny one as he dismounted and disappeared inside the house to look for himself. His tread was heavy and those left outside could hear him stomping on the floor and knocking on the walls looking for hollow places. He came outside again with a mouth full of biscuit and tossed another to his partner. "Coffee if you want some," he said holding out a cup. The skinny one took the cup and finished it off.

"Lookin' at him you think he don't never eat but he don't quit 'til every crumb's off the table," said the older man.

The skinny one tossed the empty cup to Reuben.

"You take care of that, chief," he said.

Reuben caught the cup and threw it back. The skinny one caught it, too, and might have moved on Reuben hadn't the older one told him, "Mount up." The skinny one handed the cup to Eden and did as he was told. The older one mounted up, too.

"You 'n' me, amigo," said the skinny one as he walked his horse over to where Reuben stood. "You 'n' me got us a date with destiny." Reuben stared hard at him, and the skinny one had the sense to move away. "Destiny," he called back over his shoulder.

"Be good, people," said the older one as they turned their horses back in the direction of New Hope. It was a warning.

***

Eden stayed up late that night cooking biscuits and fat pork, far more than the four of them would need for breakfast. She turned in at midnight. Joel went to bed early with *Pilgrim's Progress,* a book by a preacher from England named John Bunyan. Pritta and Sojourner slept soundly, but Reuben couldn't sleep at all. He went outside into the shadows, sat with his back against a fence post, and breathed in deeply the clean night air. The smell of the slave catchers lingered in his nostrils. He wanted to clear them out.

Reuben may have slept. He wasn't sure. But his attention was taken by the creaking leather and plodding hooves of a horse-drawn wagon approaching the mission grounds. A plain buckboard pulled by two dray horses, nothing fancy, material-ized out of the darkness and came to a stop in front of the mission house. Joel appeared at the front door with a mug of fresh, hot coffee for the teamster. Eden came out with a box filled with biscuits and fried fat pork, offered some to the driver, and put the rest in the wagon behind him. The man sat there and drank his coffee while Joel and Eden went back in-side the house. Reuben heard the scraping of a bench as it was dragged across the floor, and the sound of a board being taken up. He stood and looked through the side window, and watched as Joel helped climb out from a small hollow under the floor first a young boy about nine years of age, then a woman who must have been the boy's mother, and finally a grown man—all three Africans. They went quickly outside, where Reuben watched the man help his son and his wife into the wagon, then climbed aboard himself. The teamster, anxious to get going, snapped the reins and urged the horses south towards Mexico. Joel and Eden stood on the porch and waved goodbye. Before the wagon was out of sight, Joel took a handful of branches and swept away the tracks.

Book 2

Esau Burdock
New Mexico Territory
Spring 1834

IN THE TWENTY YEARS SINCE ESAU BURDOCK FIRST SET FOOT in the territory of New Mexico, the outpost of New Hope had grown from a dusty spot on no map at all to a small, but energetic, frontier settlement. He left New Orleans at the first hint of Spring 1814, and arrived in New Hope as the weather turned warm and hospitable, with a retinue of fifty male slaves and fifteen wagons carrying their women and children, and loaded with enough trade goods, provisions, and furniture to make a new beginning in a promising land. An armed contingent of outriders, scouts, and wranglers kept the caravan safe and heading due west from Louisiana. Esau led the way on Thor, his marvelous battle stallion. The first wagon was driven by Prospero, and carried only Gollybee and Lilly Rose as passengers, plus Esau's personal provisions. Esau had more than transcended his servitude. That trip to Natchez, Mississippi, as he neared the end of his indenture, stoked dreams he never knew he had, dreams of vast dominion and blooded horses.

He bought the business of *Hexley, Harlowe & Hunt* from the heirs, and through the continued shrewd trading of human cargo plus dead accurate speculation of other commodities— cotton, sugar, indigo, and spices—Esau became a wealthy man among wealthy men. His advice was sought, and he gave it good-naturedly but not freely, always for something in return, preferring inside information that he could use to advantage. Men marveled at his sense of business.

When he returned from Mississippi, even before the term of his servitude was up, Esau bought himself a house and installed Livy as his housekeeper. She learned to cook the foods he liked, kept the house the way he wanted, and allowed him to have her when he desired. He grew fond of her and, when she was no longer happy to sleep at the foot of his bed, con- sented to her wish for a room of her own with one stipulation: that there be no lock on her door. What could she do but agree?

Livy kept his house for nearly ten years. Esau treated her well and dressed her so she was the envy of the finest ladies in New Orleans. She was his pleasure, and rare was the moment when he was not delighted to see her. Her body remained strong, her face child-like, and she bore him no children until their ninth year. Esau was surprised at how much happiness the prospect of a child gave him. He did not bother her during her pregnancy, even doted on her, queer behavior some thought for a master towards his slave. For her part, Livy tried but failed to abort it, and so she carried a fat and healthy in- fant girl to term. She was hued like honey, with green eyes and silky hair colored like old wine, and when Esau tickled her and made her smile he knew there was no chance he would ever sell her. He named her Lilly Rose and bought Glorybee, dark and shiny as a chestnut, to help with the chores. Lilly Rose wasn't two years old when rumors of a slave rebellion reached New Orleans from the outlying plantations.

Word was the slaves would all rise up at a given time, meet at a secret destination, and, wielding their pitchforks, bludgeons, and axes, methodically slaughter all their masters before marching on the city itself. A well-armed militia quickly formed and threw up barricades blocking the roads into town. Available cannon were moved into position as well, so it seemed impossible that any of the rebels could break through. Nevertheless, Esau thought it prudent to get himself and his household as far away as possible. He sent urgent word for Livy to take Lilly Rose and Glorybee and meet him at the livery stable. Esau and his long-time coachman, Prospero, a wiry little man with the hand strength of a blacksmith, had to hitch the two horses to the carriage themselves, because all the stable boys had reported for militia duty. When Livy arrived, she handed Lilly Rose to Glorybee and climbed up to her seat. Glorybee handed Lilly Rose back and clambered up after her, where she took the child again and settled in with Lilly Rose in her arms. Esau never noticed the expression on Livy's face when she looked at him, or, if he did, in his haste it never registered. If he had he would have seen how much she detested him.

His back was to the yawning doors of the stable as he fumbled with the final buckle, when he was hit on the head from behind with a blow that dropped him to his knees. Prospero was pitched aside as Esau went down, helpless to avoid the kicks and punches that followed it seemed from every direction. He never lost complete consciousness, but he was sorely disoriented as a rope was tied around his neck and he was half dragged, half carried, and thrown into the bed of his carriage. Glorybee tried to reach Esau but was thrown from the carriage and lost hold of Lilly Rose, who screamed as she fell back against the seat. Burdock bulled himself to his feet as they tried to tie his hands behind him, but another blow dropped him to his knees again.

"Livy!" he cried, looking to her for help, but all he saw before she cracked the whip over the lunging horses was a face full of hatred. The carriage lurched forward and he swung out over the edge into space, the rope burning and tearing the flesh of his neck. It seemed that Esau would be dead in seconds, and he knew it. His last thought was of the hatred in Livy's face. His last thought...and then the rope broke from the weight of his bulk and he fell to the dirt, too dazed to move. He heard voices yelling, shots fired. They were coming to his rescue. Someone stopped the carriage. Someone else helped him to his feet. Livy had been shot dead. The musket ball shattered her breast and tore through her. Its impact knocked her back onto the seat, Lilly Rose screaming from where she'd been dropped. The pain and betrayal of the moment caused Esau to fall down in a faint. It was a horror, and when he awoke Livy's head was on a pike, her eyes bulging, her hair bloody, her face in grimace, twisted, ugly. Esau would forever wear the scars from that rope around his neck.

Journey
New Mexico
Spring, 1834

S HE WANTED TO KNOW IF SHE COULD DO IT: TICKLE THE BELLY of a fat trout and lift it from the water with her bare hand. She'd watched Reuben do it, as she had watched him do most everything these past sixteen years, though Journey had never tried it herself. But, the sap was rising in her, just as it was in all the green things on earth. The great silence of winter was finally over. Mild breezes carried aromas that were warm and sweet. The air filled with flying things. Journey had a wooden flute that Pritta made her when the snows kept them inside. She answered the birds, and the birds answered back. Insects hummed. She watched an ant crawl down her arm and across her fingers to a leaf still crinkly from the fall. She was not afraid of spiders and watched with fascination as they swung to and fro and wove their webs. Journey was delighted to be alive, and she just knew that fat fish was waiting for the touch of her hand.

The stream was swollen with melt. She chose a spot where a tree had been torn up by its roots, twisted roots that lay partially submerged and made the water swirl and eddy as it rushed by. That's where she would find her trout. She knew it, yes, she knew it would be there, resting in the thicket, feeling safe.

Journey removed her buckskin jacket, lay down half naked on the bank, gradually submerged her arm in the water, and let it move gently on its own with the current. She lay there without moving anything at all, and allowed the water to flow around her fingers as it did with the thicket of branches. Something grazed the palm of her hand and nudged her fingers. Something. Her fish! She lay without moving, and allowed her fingers to ever so slightly wave like grass under water. She felt the fish bump against them and rubbed one finger slowly along its side. She felt its scales, its slippery body, the wisp of a fin. Her heart leapt. She was sure the fish had felt it although it hadn't moved away, only moved as the water took it, and she gently, gently, stroked its side, its underside, cupped her hand, moved it under the fish, got excited, lost her patience, moved too suddenly, lost her fish. Damn! She'd heard Reuben use the word. Damn! Joel and Eden disapproved when she used it, but sometimes no other word would do. This was one of those times. Damn! She pulled her arm from the water, sat up, put on her jacket. There would be no fish today.

Journey sat on the bank and watched the water the way Reuben had taught her: that there were creatures on its surface and below it, in its cut banks, on its overhangs that lived in their own worlds with no regard for hers at all. She might invade it, take from it, disturb it, but when she left their world would return to being what it was. Her footprints would be washed away or overgrown. If she stepped in the river she left no step at all. Far as Reuben knew, nothing down there thought about anything much, but each creature breathed and became what it was meant to be. Journey breathed and wondered what she was meant to be, but it wasn't anything she had on her mind, not always, not even mostly. Mostly she just was animal like the rest of them, eating when hungry, resting when tired. She was not afraid but cautious, peaceful when not disturbed, not thoughtless, but not driven by her thoughts. Like buzzing flies; she flicked them away and went on.

Sometimes she slept at the mission, sometimes in the nearby cabin that Joel helped Reuben build, sometimes simply where she was. Journey's favorite place of all was beside a rushing mountain stream. This same spring day she fell asleep there, only to be jarred awake by the shrill whinny of an angry horse. Instantly, even before she was fully awake, she was on her feet and trotting the ridge that overlooked Wild Horse Canyon. Below her on the canyon floor were four vaqueros, two on each side of the most beautiful horse she had ever seen, the most beautiful anything she had ever seen, each vaquero with his lasso around the horse's neck. It was pure white, silver almost, like a horse in a dream—a stallion by the way it fought to get away. The way it kicked and bit no vaquero would get close to it but kept it at rope's length as they led it into the canyon. The group was bossed by a big, red bearded man on an enormous blood bay horse. Journey knew him as Esau Burdock, the richest man in the territory, breeder of horses. She'd never spoken to him, had only seen him once or twice in the settlement, but she knew from Reuben and Joel that he'd brought a stallion in from somewhere east to mate with his mares in Wild Horse Canyon.

He was looking to breed a horse that was as big as a charger, but with the agility of an Indian pony. The white stallion must be it. His voice carried to where she watched. "Cut him loose," he ordered. The four horsemen eased up on their ropes and flipped the nooses off the horse's neck. The white stallion reared and kicked at anything close, then lunged forward and raced away. Journey could see a large herd of horses watching nervously from a distance. The white stallion disappeared around a bend in the canyon and re-appeared heading straight for the other horses. The herd opened and let him through, then whirled and followed him deeper into the canyon, where all of them vanished from sight.

———◦◦◦———

Journey
New Mexico Territory
Spring, 1834

JOURNEY SAT A HORSE AS EASILY AS SHE SAT A CHAIR. AS SOON AS she could sit up by herself, Reuben placed her in front of him on his saddle. She'd lean back against him as if he were a big old armchair, warm and comfortable, but even before she could easily handle it he put her in the saddle of a horse of her own. Journey learned by doing. She had the natural balance of a red-winged blackbird on the tip of a cattail. Her first horse was a small Apache pony that was steady and didn't shy easy, and low enough to the ground, though she never did fall off but maybe once. He traded its elderly hunter a Spanish hunting knife with a bronze hilt for it. The horse wasn't young and not much to look at, though Journey loved it and cared for it the same as if it was some beauty before your eyes. She'd spend every minute she could currying its coat, cleaning its hooves, braiding its mane and tail. She even learned to shoe it. She'd have slept with it if Pritta allowed her.

As Journey grew older Reuben marveled at her skill. Even as a child she rode better than most, maybe better than any, maybe even good Reuben himself. As a child he had dreamed he was born of a horse. When he told his father, the man laughed and said it must be so. Now it was as if Journey had his blood in her veins. Surely that was true. When she was still very young, everywhere Reuben went Journey went. She rode with him to hunt buffalo, and she went to Mexico with him to steal horses. Pritta protested, but all she could do was watch them go. They went to the trapper rendezvous up to Henry's Fork, Wyoming, where she learned to trade a horse as good as any Indian. She even raced and sometimes won, though the Indians felt it was bad luck to run against her. It didn't look so good to win against a girl. It looked even worse to lose. Bad luck they muttered, but Reuben knew what was true and what was not. A horse sensed the soul and sinew on its back, and gave her all its heart in return.

In 1833 Esau Burdock called for a rendezvous in New Hope in July of the next year, 1834. That thought kept the mountain men titillated all year long. Life wintering in the mountains was so near impossible, for many of them it might've been the only thing that kept them alive. They'd descend on New Hope by the hundreds with their beaver pelts along with the Shoshone, Blackfeet, Gros Ventre, Flathead, and Apache. Vaqueros would ride up deep from Mexico, and there would be thousands of horses to race, trade, and sometimes eat. Esau promised each white man a gallon of whiskey as long as he didn't trade it to an Indian. He also promised there'd be white women there. Everything was for trade—buffalo robes, blankets, beads, gunpowder, shot, and powder horns, Hawken rifles, trade guns, saddles, dried meat, horseshoes, knives, hatchets, cooking utensils, canteens, coffee, salt. Hard money could be of little use in that piece of the world, but all the goods were. Nevertheless, when it was learned there was to be a horse race with Esau Burdock offering a leather pouch of ten gold coins to the winner, an almost unbearable excitement coursed through the settlement and worked its way into the surrounding mountains.

Some years back, Reuben and Joel had built a forge to make trade goods: knives, axes, lances, ploughshares, even cook pots. Joel also turned bowls and spoons on his lathe. Pritta made belts and moccasins and buckskin shirts, all beautifully decorated with exquisite bead work. She made canteens from dried gourds plugged with a wooden stop. Eden baked biscuits for sale with honey, fresh goat's milk from a goat she brought along, and hot coffee. Pritta also sewed together skins for a small tepee that Joel would set up next to their wagon for use as a doctor's office. Teeth gladly pulled. The morning the rendezvous was to start they loaded Joel's wagon with all their goods, and everyone except Pritta, who preferred to remain home and hidden, headed for New Hope to set up for the festivities. There'd be contests of skill, dancing, tall tales, and powerful liquor. The rendezvous would last a week, with the horse race being the final event. There was no doubt in Journey's mind that she would be in that race. She didn't care what anybody said—Indian, mountain man, vaquero, or Esau Burdock. Eden voiced her opinion. "Everybody on those horses is gonna be drunk or crazy. The girl could get hurt." Now Journey was tall, strong, all long muscle and not a shred of extra;, tough and lanky, but as much a beauty as a young woman in a king's court. That was Reuben's opinion, and don't even try to talk him out of it. "Lookit her," he said, "If she was a tree she'd be ironwood. She look like she could get hurt to you?"

"Ironwood gets cut down, too, you know," said Eden.

"Break your axe first," said Reuben.

"Save me a biscuit, Eden," said Journey, "Race like that you grow an appetite."

"Let's ride," said Joel. The wagon lurched forward. Journey and Reuben followed on horseback. Journey didn't know when she felt so excited. Just riding next to her made Reuben happy. She was something, that girl. She didn't belong to him, but she didn't belong to nobody else either. Free as the sun and moon. Free as air.

———— ∞∞∞ ————

Esau Burdock saw them ride into town and set up shop near where the finish line would be. They were the religious people, but the girl wasn't theirs, didn't look like either one of them, taller, lighter than them. He didn't trust those two. She wasn't the old Indian's either. Reuben Moon. Wasn't that his name? Looked to have some Mexican in him. *Who was she?* Esau wondered. What was this queer feeling come over him when he looked at her? He'd go over later and talk to them. Be friendly. Right now he had too much to do. There were a thousand men and three thousand horses coming into the settlement, most of them here already, camping up and down the river, spread out all around the place, Indians building lodges, bearded men with tents made of skins. Most of them had beards so full they looked like used brooms. The white women were on the way, two wagons of them. Esau chuckled when he thought what a busy week they had coming. Should be a good week. The trappers would have their memories and their lies. Esau liked to listen to them spin their stories, even though most were full of shit.

A voice interrupted his thoughts. "Mr. Burdock," someone said. "We caught this dinge in Mexico. Shoulder brand says he's one of yours." It was the two slave catchers with a string of horses and an old colored man with a rope around his neck, looked like he was about to die. How'd they walk up on him without him seeing?

"What you want us to do with him?" the older one asked.

"See if the Indians'll take him. I won't get no more out of him," said Esau.

"You owe us for him," said the younger, the one they called Cottonmouth because the inside of his mouth being all grayish-white. This was the first time Esau had ever heard him speak. Usually, the older one did the talking.

"See what you can get for him then keep it," said Esau.

"He's too old and wore out for much," said Cottonmouth.

"A jug of whiskey be just about right," said the older man. Cottonmouth smiled and showed his pointy teeth.

"One of them white women be good, too," he said. "They here yet?"

"Take the whiskey," said Esau. "The women do their own talking."

"They here yet?" Cottonmouth asked again.

"You see them? Then they ain't here yet," said Esau.

"What about the dinge?" asked the older man, the one called Meshach.

"You heard me once. Trade him to the Indians," Esau repeated. "He's good for squaw work."

"He'll be dead soon," offered Cottonmouth.

"Then he won't eat much, will he?" said Esau

Cottonmouth wanted to know, "What we goin' t'do with him, Meshach?"

He was asking about the old slave, who right then was kneeling in the dirt spitting up blood.

"Get up on your feet, goddamn you!" ordered Cotton-mouth. "I can't do nothin' with you on your knees." The old man staggered to his feet. He wobbled, but managed to stay there as his body wracked with a cough. "You hobble the horses," Cottonmouth said to Meshach. "I got a idea." He checked the rope around the old man's neck and tugged on it. "Let's go," he said and began walking down the street. The old man stumbled and followed.

Eden saw them coming first. "Joel," she said and caught her husband's attention. Journey looked up, too. They watched as the skinny man with the grayish skin and filed teeth headed their way, with the sick Negro barely able to walk on the rope behind him. Journey looked around for Reuben, but he had disappeared somewhere into the crowd.

"Got a sick one here," announced Cottonmouth.

"Get that rope off his neck!" ordered Joel.

"I will if you take him," answered Cottonmouth. "dinge needs a doctor."

Joel rushed out and removed the noose from the slave.

"You goin' to take him?" asked Cottonmouth. "Get him better so he's worth somethin'?"

The old slave could barely continue standing.

"Help me with him," Joel said to Cottonmouth. The two men helped him into Joel's doctor's tent and lay him down on a buffalo robe. Eden came in with a cup of coffee and a biscuit. She put the cup to the old man's lips, but he was too weak to eat or drink.

"I'll take that if he don't want it," said Cottonmouth. Journey appeared in the door of Joel's tent. Cottonmouth smiled his pointy toothed smile and said, "How're you, missy?"

"How much you want for him?" Joel asked.

"A biscuit and some of that coffee," answered Cotton-mouth.

"Take it and go," said Eden as she handed him the biscuit and coffee.

Cottonmouth hammered the meaty edge of his right hand onto the palm of his left, signifying a bargain had been reached.

"You're good people," he said and turned to go. He leered and gave Journey a wink.

"Maybe you 'n' me'll have a dance." With that he left. Eden wet a cloth and placed it on the old man's burning fore-head.

"You're free," she said. The old man smiled weakly, then shut his eyes and never opened them again. By dark he was dead.

———∞∞∞———

What a good week it was! Esau oversaw it all from the back of his blood bay warhorse. Thor was getting older but so was Esau, who thought that if he died first he wanted to be like one of them Chinese emperors and have his horse buried with him—him and Thor, ride into the next world and beyond that. The weather held. Fist fights was an obligation you had if you was to call yourself a mountain man, but gun play was minimal, and you never heard of a fist fight between a white man and an Indian. Indians didn't believe in fist fights. They wanted to get it over quick with a war club to the head. Every so often somebody'd get so drunk they'd think they were Jim Bowie. Back a few years he'd become famous for disembowel-ing three men in a knife fight after an occurrence called the Sandbar Duel. Bowie was an attendant on one side, and after the duelers quit the field the attendants took on each other. Bowie was wounded by a gunshot but still managed to gut one, split the skull of another, and take the head off the third was what you heard. After that everybody began carrying knives long as their right arm, something of the tall tale in that but not too much. They wore them strapped to their leg or hanging down their back, and got fancier as the years went by. Jim and his brother, Rezin, made a fortune on them.

The only ones certain to make real money out of all this were the two wagonloads of painted women, not one of whom turned out to be white. Had to be cash, gentlemen, or you could cast your seed upon the waters. Reuben and Joel got real money for their goods as well, though they would take essentials in trade like salt and coffee, too, sometimes a particularly fine buffalo robe or a lion fang or a bear claw necklace. Eden kept the hot coffee and biscuits coming and never charged a thing, but the traffic she brought to the wagon was well worth it. What Esau stood to get out of all this was a boatload of prestige. It would ensure his reputation as the most powerful man in the territory, without a doubt, maybe all New Mexico. Even with all the excitement, even with all the festivities and things to look at, all Journey cared about was the race at the end of the week. She spent her time studying the horses and finding out which ones would race, and she ignored all the offers she got to meet some man in his tent. Most of them were missing teeth and smelled worse than winterkill, not that anything else would have mattered. When Esau got word she was going to race, he had all the excuse he needed to stroll over to the wagon.

Stroll over on horseback actually. More impressive that way. He knew who they were, although he had never passed a word with any of them, and he was sure they knew who he was. Everybody did. He was Esau Burdock, citizen of these States of a United America, owner of all a man could see, breeder of horses that flew on earth, worked his people hard but kept them dry and fed them good. Esau didn't think God worked in such mysterious ways. He came to this country to save himself from a hanging, though even then some might say he was handed a choice: After all, they could've just hung him, clapped and laughed while he danced on air, and that would've been that. He'd have danced the quadrille with his old mum in Hell. Instead, he was handed a business opportunity, and he had the vision and fortitude to make the most of it. That's right. He could've been hung but here he was: the Almighty's example of what a man can do.

Now take that girl, tall and strong, fair in mind and body. Who was she? No Mexican or Apache in her, so she wasn't Reuben Moon's, although the way she acted towards him you might think she was. The squaw who whelped her had no nose and never walked among the rest of us. No blood there. Those two religious, she wasn't theirs either, both of them too dark and short, but "Journey" was the kind of name they might've come up with. They were religious, so did they know something? She watched him as he rode up, not him so much as the horse, Thor the war horse, black as my heart. That made him laugh. Reuben Moon stepped forward beside her as if to protect her. Somebody his age. What was he thinking? The woman stopped what she was doing, poured a cup of coffee and held it out to him with a smile, same way he took it. Why not? The man, Joel, came out of the tent, his doctor's office.

"How are you, Mr. Burdock?" Joel asked, and put his hand out for a shake. Good grip for a little man.

"They tell me you pulled enough teeth so far to make a necklace," said Burdock.

"Pulled a few," said Joel. "How 'bout one of yours?"

Was he joking?

"I want a tooth pulled I tie it to a door and kick the damn thing shut," said Esau.

"No whiskey first?" asked Joel with a grin.

"Only about a jug of it," answered Esau with a grin of his own. He turned smiling to Journey. "Got all my teeth but one, young lady, and that in back so you don't see it. Comes from chewing your food. Hey, Reuben, you can stand back. I'm not gonna bite her." Reuben stayed where he was. What could happen? But still, he felt what he felt.

"You're up against Shoshone, Blackfeet, Crow, white men so mean they breathe fire," he addressed Journey. "You got no fear?"

"They won't get close enough," she answered. She wasn't bragging. She was just saying what she knew to be true. Her voice was strong like her manner. If she had fear she certainly didn't show it.

"Where's your horse?" Esau wanted to know. Journey pointed out a good sized paint hitched to a wagon wheel. She and Reuben had recently brought up a string from Mexico, and she had traded two to an Apache for this one.

"Skinny legs," said Esau.

"He can run flat out two miles and not take a breath," she countered.

"Well," said Esau, "That's what he's going to have to do. Those men ain't goin' to lose easy."

"They can lose easy. They can lose hard," she said, "But lose is what they're goin' to do."

"Who are you, girl?" he asked. His question and the way it shot out of his mouth, unplanned, unexpected, shocked even him.

Journey pointed to Reuben then to Joel and Eden.

"I'm his, and I'm theirs," she answered.

"Then you ain't nobody's," he cracked.

"I'm anybody's I want to be," she snapped back, "'Cept yours."

Esau didn't like that. It made him angry, but it made him more, something he didn't understand, something like being clawed quick by a fast cat. But the feeling went by real fast, like when you jerk your hand away.

"Only thing writ in stone be the Ten Commandments," he said.

She was gone by the time Esau turned his horse around.

———— ∞∞ ————

The race course started right outside the settlement and headed for the river, crossed the narrows and carried up a steep bluff on the other side, turned around at a stand of red pine, crossed the narrows again, blazed across the flats, and finished in the middle of the main street. Two miles front to back. There were a hundred of them spread out along the starting line, spitting, cursing, hollering insults up and down the line, jostling for position, trying to knock the other riders off balance. Journey held her position and wasn't one bit intimidated. Her focus was on the river a mile ahead. She saved her horse's energy by keeping him as still as she could. She was in charge and he knew it, stayed calm, ready to spring, ready to take wing. Reuben said to himself, *Let 'em holler*. Wasn't any such as these goin' to out run his Journey, and if they hurt her, wasn't any goin' to outrun him.

None of these lame brains made a bit of difference to Journey. Joel had read to her from a book about a horse with wings that could soar above the earth, and that was the feeling she had when her horse was running flat out under her. She soared above the earth, and that was where Journey loved to be.

"Hey, you, Journey!" A man's voice cut through the tumult. "Journey, goddamnit, over here!" A sharp whistle bit her ear like a bee sting. She looked down the line and saw him, only a few riders away. Hadn't noticed before. He was smiling at her. The one with the pointy teeth. "Hey, I win I get a dance!"

"You win you'll be dancin' with yourself. Shake your own hand and say, 'Pleased to meetcha,'" quipped Journey.

"Just a kiss then." He didn't give up.

"You wish."

"I do." He winked and blew her one. Journey stuck her finger down her throat and made a gagging sound.

"That mean you love me?" he asked.

"Puke," she said with disdain, turned away and waited for Esau to fire the shot to start the race. He was behind the line not far from where she was.

"Mark," he shouted. "Set." He waited. The bantering died out. Tension built. The horses felt it, too, as anxious to get going as the men on their backs. He fired, and the line leapt forward.

For the first few yards the animals ran fairly even, stayed in a clump for a few yards more, then began to stretch out on the flat as they hit their strides. When Journey and her horse reached their rhythm, they broke out of the pack but were still with a clutch of others that had done the same thing. Journey was in the race, but so were they. The lead group was still running together as they hit the river narrows, but the water weeded them out and Journey fell back. She gained speed on the other side of the river, and by the time she turned back and reached it again she was back in the race. Her horse handled the crossing with ease this time, reached the flats still in the race, and opened up. A dozen jockeyed for position, first one pulling ahead, then another. Journey held the lead for a few strides, then lost it but stayed running with the pack. The finish line was in sight, maybe a minute away. The rider to her left caught up to her and whipped his horse in a fury. It was the snake with the ashy skin and filed down teeth. Damn if she was going to lose to him. She rein whipped her horse and had it going as fast as it could go, but the moron stayed with her. They thundered towards New Hope. Journey was still in the race. Until. Her horse, running way beyond itself, stumbled and went down, and Journey was kicked unconscious by the horse behind her. She never saw the finish.

You'd have thought he was a young man the way Reuben leapt to his horse and raced bareback towards where Journey lay. The winner had already crossed the finish line as Reuben rode past the stragglers in the opposite direction. Nobody else had trampled her as far as he could see, but Journey wasn't moving and still wasn't when he reached her. Her paint grazed calmly nearby as if nothing had happened. Reuben didn't know how Joel had got there so fast, but there he was kneeling beside him. Journey's eyes were open but rolled back in her head. The color had drained from her face, so it looked like a mask made to keep evil away, but she was still breathing, soft as if she slept, but uneven. She would breathe and then not breathe, breathe and then not breathe. There was a large welt on her forehead where the hoof had connected with her head, but no blood anywhere. Reuben placed his hands on either side of her head, and stared into her eyes as if willing life into her.

"Careful," said Joel. "Let me see her." Reuben moved aside and Joel felt the girl's pulse that was still strong. He took a vial of salts from his pocket and held it under her nose. For a few eternal seconds her breathing remained shallow, but then she snorted mightily as if coming up for air from a deep pool, and right after pulled her head away. Her eyes came into focus as she looked around her.

"Did I win?" she asked.

"Depends on how you look at it," answered Joel. "You're still alive."

"Then I didn't win?" she asked as if disgusted with herself. "Who did?"

"Didn't see," answered Reuben.

"Not that ugly one?"

"Didn't see, I said."

"All we saw was your horse go down," said Joel.

"How is she?" asked Journey.

"Like nothin' happened," said Reuben. "She's over there."

Journey raised herself up on her elbows to look.

"You'd best take it easy, young lady," warned Joel. "Let's get you back to the tent and keep our eyes on you for a while."

Reuben helped her to her feet. She felt shaky and hung into him.

"Feel like I got no feet," said Journey.

"You got everything you was born with," said Reuben, now in a much better mood. He helped her onto his horse and got on behind her to hold her steady.

"You take her horse," he said to Joel, "We'll see you back there."

All the people ranged along the way applauded Journey as she went by. The painted women from the two wagons cheered louder than anybody. The weasel with the pointy teeth did a waltz step across the road. When Reuben and Journey reached the medical tent Esau Burdock was waiting for them. So was Eden.

"You sure did give us a scare," said Eden. "I heated up some milk for you and mixed a little honey in it." She smiled and said with relief, "Good for falling off a horse. All the best doctor books say so."

Esau smiled and asked, "You back in the land of the living?"

"Soon's I get some sleep I'll let you know," she said as Reuben helped her down.

"You made it a race. I'll hand you that," Esau said.

"Got your money's worth?" she asked.

"More than," he answered.

"Who won?" she wanted to know as Reuben led her into the tent.

"Some Apache from down river."

"Not that weasely one?"

Esau shook his head.

"Cottonmouth looked back to see what happened to you and lost. You got somethin' against him?" asked Esau.

"I'm workin' on it," said Journey

"Let's get you inside," said Eden.

"Give me a second," said Esau as he dug into his pocket, pulled out a gold coin, and handed it to Journey.

"What for?" she asked.

"The sun's out. I'm feeling generous today," he answered.

"I guess so," she said.

As the tent flap closed behind her, he said, "Listen to your doctor, child. See you get well."

Journey was strong and got well quickly, though not quickly enough for her. Joel insisted she rest a few days before becoming active again, at least until a persistent headache went away, but she hated being still and shut in. She had such energy it was near impossible for her to stifle it. Why, it was summer out there! How could she resist it? Life began in the spring and ended in the fall, but summer! Summer was when the world

was most full! Summer thrilled her with the concussive wonder of its thunderstorms, made her drunk with the scents of its
flowers, delighted her with the songs of its birds, made her
want to twirl round and round in the heat of the sun until the
whole world and all its sky whirled around her head. She wondered, "Were there insects on the moon? Are moles sad because
they cannot see the sun? Why are there so many different
colors in the meadow? Why do insects buzz and birds whistle?
Why? Why? Why?" Spring was a time of awakening. Fall
blazed in splendor designed to hide death. Winter pressed
down with the bulk of an old bear. But summer was a rich
blood that flowed in the veins, a sweet pudding, a joyous
dance where everything and everyone had a partner.

Reuben had put up his smooth bore musket and traded a
smoked saddle of elk, two knives, and a hatchet for two
Hawken rifles, guns that could reach out two hundred yards
with deadly accuracy. One had a shorter barrel than the other.
That was Journey's. When the time came they would hunt
meat for everyone else. That was just dandy with Joel, who
didn't like to kill anything anyway. He'd do the pigs, but took
no pleasure in it. Reuben promised her lessons when Joel gave
his say so. In the meantime, Reuben made her a slingshot from
a buffalo tail. All day she practiced from the porch hitting tar-
gets on the fence. Journey wouldn't admit it, but Joel knew
when she got a little dizzy and made her sit down and rest.

When Journey was younger, a child less than half of what
she was now, one hot Summer day when the river was lazy and
everything moved more slowly than usual, she was lying in a
meadow on her back, arms and legs outstretched, her mouth
watering from the scent of wild onions, watching the billowy
clouds, whiter than chicken eggs, shift their shapes, she suddenly realized she could understand what the birds were saying. Journey was no good at tweeting and whistling, so she

couldn't answer them back, but they weren't especially talking to her directly anyway but amongst themselves, tree to tree. She simply understood them. Their voices entered her head the way her dreams did, and she understood them. Then, right there and then, she heard the squirrels chattering—*tch-tch-tch-tch tch tch*—and she knew that she could actually talk to them. So she did. *Tch tch tch*. How long she did this she did not know, but they came to her, slowly, each bit of ground a little closer until two of them stood next to her and chattered in her ears. She chattered back and they crawled up her arms, over her chest, down her legs, until she burst out in laughter at the joy of it all, and they scampered away. When she grew older she couldn't do this anymore, but while she was young she could talk them out of trees and feed them from her hand. They chattered and scattered, but they always came back. Until she was older. When Journey was older it became horses.

Once she was allowed on horseback again, she saddled up and rode to the rim of Wild Horse Canyon to see if she could spot the herd ruled by the white stallion Esau had put there the past spring. She knew she'd have to wait through the end of summer, then the fall, then the winter, to see any new foals from the mares the stallion no doubt had already mounted. Journey just didn't know if she could wait that long. She'd have to, though, wouldn't she? No way to change the nature of a horse, so she'd simply have to be patient.

But sitting there as she was, so still, moving no more than a pile of rocks, something caught her attention and held her as much as anything ever had. A mountain lion climbed towards the rim of the canyon. Was it the same one she'd seen before? That one had sat on the rim of the fresh crater and watched her climb up. They'd held each other's eyes before the cat turned and disappeared. Now a cat was climbing towards her, halfway up, nimbly picking its way over and around the jagged rocks. She was way above it, so it hadn't caught her scent, and the sight of it made her hold her breath. She made not a single move. Journey was amazed at how quickly it climbed such a steep slope, a canyon wall near straight up and down. The cat kept coming, close enough to see her now if she moved. But she didn't. She did not move, and because she did not move she saw that the lion walked with a limp, favoring its right front paw. It was not more than fifty feet away when it sensed her presence, stopped and stared right at her, held her eyes for what seemed forever, then ran on an incline across the face of the canyon wall in the opposite direction from where she sat, bounded up over the canyon rim and was gone.

Journey yearned for winter to pass quickly, but winter had its ways and would not be hurried. Meshach and Cottonmouth showed up at the mission again hunting runaways, but Reuben and Journey had long since gone with an African family to Mexico. Cottonmouth wanted to know where Journey was, but she was nowhere close at the time hunting big horn sheep with Reuben in the mountains on their way back home. Sheep meat would be a welcome change to the deer and elk they hunted in the north. Reuben had seen to it that she knew her rifle as well as she knew her horse. The Hawken was top of the line, still single shot and muzzle loaded but with an octagonal barrel and lovely walnut stock that fit her shoulder nicely and against which she rested her cheek when taking aim. It fired a heavy caliber ball that gave her shoulder quite a punch, though her concentration was so intense she barely felt it. Journey became so adept she could fire, reload—powder, patch, ball, ramrod— and fire again in twenty seconds. She took her first ram with a single shot to the heart that dropped it in place. Reuben did the same. They wrapped the meat in wet muslin from Mexico to keep it fresh, immersed it in cold streams when they camped for the night, and beat the first snowfall home. The first snow-fall was particularly heavy for that early in the winter. When November came and brought the snow with it the day she was born, there may well have been another rain of fire in the sky, though this year it was too overcast to see a single star.

"Where was I born? Who was my mother?" Often Journey put these thoughts from her mind, but this time of year she could not. It was winter and she had to be still, and when she was still she wondered these things. She wondered these things even though she had asked and been given answers. Reuben and Pritta did not live together as man and wife, although they shared the same cabin and raised Journey as their own. But she did not come from them. Reuben was a mix blood of Apache and Mexican, son of a cibolero, a buffalo hunter. She did not look like him. Pritta was pure Apache. Journey did not look like her. Journey, with her tall, strong, slender body and hair so blonde as to be nearly white, Journey did not look like anyone. She asked Reuben, "Did you know my mother?"

"Pritta is your mother," he answered.

"The woman I come from," she insisted.

"I didn't know her," replied Reuben, "She was with the Co-manche in the north when she died giving birth. The Coman-che were scared of you. They thought you were some kind of spirit and intended to leave you in the forest. I thought you were a little piece of gold, so I took you and brought you to Pritta."

She fingered the small figurine at her throat of the man sitting cross-legged with a fat belly and a smiling face carved from a green stone about the size of an acorn. One hand with two fingers was raised in greeting. The stone was not turquoise and came from somewhere else. It was on a gold chain and hung around her neck and between her breasts, always hidden by her buckskin shirt.

"Does this have magic?" she once asked.

"Yes," Reuben had replied.

"What does it do?" she wanted to know.

"It keeps you safe," answered Reuben.

"Did she give it to me?"

"Who?"

"The woman," she asked.

"No," said Reuben, "The Comanches did. They took it from her neck, and I put it around yours."

"Did you lie down with her?"

"No."

"But you're my father?"

"Yes."

That was all Reuben would say and all Journey knew.

————— ∞∞∞ —————

Journey was not the only one whose winter thoughts ventured to uncomfortable places. Esau Burdock sat in an over-sized black walnut chair recently reupholstered in soft, tanned deer hide, his feet up on a matching ottoman, both items gotten years ago from a once magnificent hacienda in Mexico that had fallen into disrepair. The arms of the chair were wide enough to hold a glass of port or brandy, cases of which were regularly shipped to him up river from New Orleans. A fire blazed in the fireplace built with stone taken from the original derelict structure and mantled with oak, carved and scrolled by a master craftsman, wide enough to hold a small tree. Esau had eaten mutton for dinner, and this evening drank brandy. He was fifty-four years old and had come to consider himself an enlightened man. His slaves were well fed and kept warm. He allowed them to hunt for fresh meat and keep plots of vegetables that nourished them. He did not trade in slaves anymore, didn't need to because generations flourished under his care. Esau had come to believe that slavery exists because it is best for the African, constituted and made as he is. If it does not best promote his welfare and happiness as well as that of his master, then it ought to be abolished. But it is a Truth undeniable that the African was created to serve, and the master to see that this service was beneficial to all. Esau believed this and was proud of his place in God's world.

Why then, at this juncture of his life, when he had come so far, was he still troubled? If his mother could see him now, would she even know who he was? He rubbed the scars burnt into his neck by the rope and thought again of Livy. She appeared in his dreams. How could Livy have turned on him when she did? The hatred on her face as she fixed him the instant before she snapped the whip–where had it come from? He had dressed her well and fed her well, and was more than happy with the way she ran his house. Rarely did he reprimand her. But once did he beat her. She did what she wanted, but then she had wanted him dead; she almost succeeded, and her betrayal continued to eat at his core. She had gnawed into his heart like a weevil. He would picture her face with only a touch of the African, barely a touch, a beauty in all aspects, and a delight in her ways, the manner of her walk, the way she sang when she worked. Wasn't that the sound of happiness? But in his dreams she rode away from him on horseback and never looked back. He did not doubt that it was Livy. He knew her dress—one he'd bought her—the way she wore her hair, the set of her shoulders. It was surely Livy. Why had she come into his life again? Why had the dreams returned? With all his wealth,

Esau was a lonely man. He would admit this to no one, barely to himself, but there were nights like this when he thought about his losses. He raised their child, Lilly Rose, and then she was gone as well. When Livy left his dream, Lilly Rose appeared. She'd been found in the forest, all bones, and buried where they found her. Creatures had fed on her soft skin. Esau did not want to look, but neither she nor Livy would leave him alone. Both been gone a long time, but now they'd come back.

——————⊗⊗⊗——————

The mountain lion was another creature having difficulty weathering a cruel winter. Although it was a big cat—eight feet in length and approaching two hundred pounds—it was aging at nearly eleven years old, a lifetime for most panthers in the wild. A further factor was the wound it had sustained to its right forepaw when it tore its way out of the teeth of a steel trap. This had happened when the cat was younger, and he adapted to it; but still, as he grew older it could be a nuisance when pulling down full grown deer or elk. Much of its prey was now smaller. Still, it was the beast, the destroyer. It remained able to defend its territory; no other cat would dare approach it. But due to its age its range had decreased from more than a hundred square miles to less than fifty, and while it could still power its way through deep snow it took more effort than it had when he was younger.

Today it lay under an overhang sheltered from a heartless wind, and looked out across its range towards the ranch. Regardless of the stock in its pastures and in its yards the cat remained too cautious to approach it. Humans were there, and it knew not to trust them. Along with the sounds made by the stock, the cat heard their words carried by the wind and knew to stay away. But the difference between now and then, when he was younger, was that now he considered it. Sheep and cattle and horses all had their young, and today they came to the big cat's attention. When he caught their scent his eyes narrowed, his tail with its black tip twitched, and a low rumble emanated from his throat. The sound of a child's laughter came to him as a tinkle. Humans had young, too. He heard it again and bared his fangs.

Journey
Spring
1835

THIS PAST WINTER HAD BEEN BRUTAL BUT SHORT. THE SNOWS had cleared by the beginning of March, and although the temperatures were still low the snow kept its distance. Only the tops of the mountains were dusted. Animals gave birth, and forage was easier. Buzzards rode the thermals looking for winterkill. Bears were on the move. White furred ermines emerged from their dens as stoats with brown coats. Birds built nests and began laying eggs. Journey emerged as well. Her hair was longer—she had to push some of it out of her eyes—a little bit curlier, maybe even a bit lighter. Her skin was pale due to lack of sunlight. Her body had filled out since the fall and felt not altogether familiar. How could her legs have gotten so long without her knowing it? She felt earthbound, but the spring air energized her, and what she wanted most was to be up in the mountains where the air was even cleaner and clearer, and where she stood on top of the world. She headed straight for her paint in the corral, where he'd been penned up most of the winter. He snorted when he saw her, eager to go, too. She led him out of the corral, closed the gate behind them, and leapt to his bare back. No saddle for him. Her horse wanted freedom as much as she did. He sensed what she intended, and headed for the mountains without being told.

Winter had been a time for dreams, and most of Journey's were of horses. In her dreams she ran on foot with the herd in Wild Horse Canyon. Horses were all around her, and she was as swift as they were. She could run with them forever.

Journey rode her horse up the ridge overlooking the canyon, then along the ridgeline that gradually sloped down through jagged boulders to the canyon floor. Even on horseback she felt so tiny amidst the immensity of it all. She was part of it, and she knew that, but just a part of it. Today the sun shone a gentle light on her world and helped her find the way, just as it did for the other creatures of the canyon. From a granite shelf high up on one of the cliffs the lion watched as well. Its eyes were amber, wide, unblinking. A low growl rumbled deep down in its throat.

Journey rode along the canyon floor staying alert for signs of the herd. She rounded a bend, and her horse knew they were there before she did. He whinnied, and a whinny came back. She spotted the herd down canyon, spread out and grazing peacefully. The stallion, white as the full moon, stood guard with massive chest and long, powerful legs. A small band of mares and foals seemed to be grazing in her direction. Journey dismounted, hitched her mount to a cedar sapling, made her way in a crouch from rock to rock, and hunkered down in a clump of juniper.. One foal wandered from the band and grazed towards the juniper, unaware of Journey's presence. The girl had never seen anything so beautiful in all her life. The foal. The little horse. A colt was a chestnut of deep burnished gold with flaxen tail and mane, a white blaze, blue eyes, and four white socks. Sunlight wrapped around the young horse and made it glow. The colt seemed a statue sculpted from precious metal. Its mother, a dark, nearly black chestnut, grazed nearby.

Journey stayed still as stump as the chestnut colt continued in her direction. It grazed right up to the clump of juniper. The girl and the horse were eyeball to eyeball, so close together she could feel its heartbeat as her own, so close that when the wind shifted the young horse pulled up its head in alarm. Its nostrils flared. The little colt came straight up off the ground, and Journey, startled, fell backwards. The great white stallion trumpeted in alarm, whirled, and drove his herd further down canyon. Foals raced awkwardly beside their mothers. The stallion appeared to be everywhere. He nipped the flank of a lagging mare, bared his teeth at another. The colt wheeled around to follow the herd and ran easily on its fringe. The horses raced past a narrow arroyo without breaking stride, but the colt turned its head to look at the girl and vanished into the arroyo itself as the herd kept on without him.

Journey crept out from the clump of juniper and made her way slowly towards the arroyo. Could she sneak up on the colt and get close to him again? Her thoughts were ruptured by a hideous roar and a squeal of terror. She forgot all caution and ran to the mouth of the arroyo, where she saw a huge lion ride the colt to the ground. Journey's screams grabbed the lion's attention. It stopped its attack but remained standing over the colt, bared its terrible fangs, and growled at the girl. The young horse didn't move, but the lion did. Stiff legged, its ears flat to its head, the beast stepped across the colt's body and moved deliberately on Journey. She stood there, terrified. Reuben would say, "Don't turn! Don't run!" and, hearing his voice, she held onto herself, pulled her slingshot from her belt and whipped a stone off the beast's head. It stopped him only for an instant, though in that instant the deep brown chestnut mare raced into the arroyo and attacked the cat. She reared over him in a fury and kicked his head with a sharp front hoof. The lion shook himself but didn't back off, faced the mare, eyes thin as razors. The mare spun around and kicked out with both rear legs, missed, spun around once more and flailed with both front hooves. The cat had not grown older without good reason. It dodged the hooves, and charged underneath the mare to her exposed belly. It rolled onto its back, buried its fangs in the soft flesh under her heart, and raked her midsection with the claws of all four feet. The mare charged forward, but the lion held on. She screamed with pain, fell to the ground, rolled on her back, her hooves still flailing. The big cat's jaws closed on her throat, clamped down, ground, tore. The mare's neck twisted grotesquely. She jerked with the agony of death, and lay still.

The beast backed off her body. It limped but held its ground, turned, and faced the girl. Journey raised her arms high above her head, screamed and screamed—"Get out! Get away!"—but the cat snarled and started forward, blood on its fangs and claws. Journey picked up a larger rock and fired it at the beast's head. It winced, and this time retreated and dashed to a ledge on the arroyo's wall. The lion stood still for a minute and boldly appraised this creature who had stung him as if imprinting this curious thing in its memory, storing the appraisal away for some future time. A few seconds passed, and then the lion snarled and limped off.

Journey ran to the colt. It made a feeble effort to rise and run but could only shudder and lie still. She gently but firmly stroked the young horse's flank and examined the four ugly gashes that ran the length of its delicately arched neck, over the side of his jaw and upward across his forehead. She put her ear to the colt's nose. He was still breathing.

"I'm not gonna let you die," she said.

She took a quick drink of water from her canteen, and poured a substantial amount onto the ground beside her. When the dirt became mud, Journey used it to plaster the colt's wounds. She held the young horse's head and stroked him.

"I'll take care of you. You'll be fine," she said. The colt shuddered again and opened his eyes. He tried to stand, but couldn't. Journey took an apple from her pocket and held it to the horse's mouth, but he was too weak to do more than sniff it. Journey held him until the mud dried, then she washed it off and applied wet mud again. She continued to do this all day long until the sun went down, then she made a bow from the rawhide strip she wore around her head and built a fire. Once again she held an apple to the colt's mouth, but he was still too weak to eat it. Journey ate it herself, settled back against a rock, and continued to hold the colt's head, stroke him and talk to him while the night went by. Some time later her paint, still hobbled, found her. She dug a hole and poured in some water. The big horse drank and was able to eat an apple

When dawn came the colt again refused an apple, but was able to drink some water. He seemed reassured that another horse was close by. Journey plastered the colt with mud again, and continued to nurse him throughout the second day. She knew that Joel and Eden would be worried about her, maybe Pritta was, too, but she didn't think Reuben would. Maybe a little. Not much. Anyway, she didn't want to think about it. Her hands were full of horse. That's what she was doing.

The evening of the second day, Journey built another fire. Her canteen was nearly empty, and so she worried what she would do without water. But a heavy spring rain fortuitously soaked the area that night. Large drops of it danced and sizzled on the fire until they put it out. Journey would be cold until the sun came up, but at least there was water. The colt stuck out its tongue to catch the raindrops. There would be mud in the morning, and she let her bandanna soak through so she'd have enough for herself for another day. After that? She didn't know. Maybe it would rain again.

The morning of the third day, Journey again held an apple to the colt's mouth. This time, to her great joy, he smelled it, licked it, nibbled on it, then ate every bit. She fed him another, and he ate that one, too. Afterwards, he seemed to want to stand. He did so, shakily, and Journey helped him to his feet. The colt would bear the scars from the lion for the rest of his life, but he would live.

Journey took the hobbles off her paint, and led it out of the arroyo to a stream in the canyon full and rushing from the rain. The colt followed them. Journey got on her hands and knees and thrust her head into the cool, rejuvenating water. The colt drank beside her, and so did the paint. The young horse nuzzled the girl, and she smiled. Yes. He would live. Journey plastered the colt with mud one final time, then mounted her paint and rode to where the trail went up the ridge and out of the canyon. The colt followed until Journey started up the ridge, and then it stopped and whinnied softly.

"You come with me if you like," said Journey, but the colt stayed where he was. "I'll be back," she said. She put her fingers into her mouth the way Reuben had taught her and whistled.

"You hear that you come running," she told him, and continued up the trail while the colt watched her go.

Pritta, Joel, Eden—they had all been worried about her; three days in the mountains was a long time to be away. Even Reuben had been concerned, although he had faith that Journey knew what she was doing. However, if she hadn't returned when she did, he would have gone out after her. When she told them where she'd been and what had happened they were no less concerned, especially when she stated she was going back. She asked Joel for a salve to put on the colt's wounds, and asked Eden for a sack to put in a supply of biscuits and apples. Journey also asked Eden if she could borrow a ceramic feeding cup that Eden kept in case an infant could not be nursed by its mother and no wet nurse could be found, but these were deemed too delicate, so Reuben came up with a better idea. He had a hollow bull's horn that he often used as a powder horn. He made a nipple or teat out of leather that he attached to the small end of the horn. Milk was poured into the large end (sweetened cow's milk for the colt), with the nipple end to be placed in the horse's mouth. Reuben filled a bucket with milk and enclosed it with a piece of tanned hide. The real problem was transporting the milk to the canyon.

Word had reached them that a lion's tracks had been seen on Esau Burdock's property, but there was no kill and no one spotted the lion. However, it was a big one, and its right forepaw had appeared to have suffered serious damage. Reuben felt it was the same one; Journey knew so. He told her, "Next time you take your rifle."

"I will," she replied.

Joel gave Journey the salve, Eden a sack of apples and biscuits. Reuben had her wear his hunting knife, and Journey took a blanket, a buffalo hide on which to sleep, extra water, and a supply of jerky as she set out again the next day for Wild Horse Canyon. She held the bucket with both hands on the saddle in front of her.

"How long you be gone?" asked Eden.

"I'll be fine," Journey assured her, although none of the adults felt easy about it. They all knew the girl had no immediate plans to come back in. They might have been even more worried if they had gotten word that two nights ago there had been a confirmed kill at Esau Burdock's.

The kill had been a little colored boy, a young slave by the name of Abel not yet nine years old, small for his age. He lived with his mother in a cabin near a corral where the newborn lambs were kept. It was Abel's job to watch over them. It wasn't yet bedtime when they heard a racket from the corral: lambs bleating, deeper bleats from the ewes. Abel and his mother went out to see about all the commotion. They entered, but at first, they saw nothing, only the sheep milling around. Abel's mother was looking the other way when she heard him scream, turned around, and saw a lion about to pounce on him. She screamed as well, though the lion acted as if she wasn't there and jumped on the boy, took his head in its mouth, and began to shake him. The woman leapt on the lion's back and tried to claw its eyes and pull it from her son, but the beast shook her off. She saw her son trying to crawl away, but the lion locked its jaws on the boy's midsection, jumped the fence, and disappeared into the darkness. A search for Abel found his body under a bush, partially eaten, and covered with grass, leaves, dirt, sticks, and stones.

Abel's mother was inconsolable and not worth a damn since the boy was killed. Had this been years ago, Esau would have whipped some sense into her, but he had mellowed somewhat with age and let her be, knowing she'd come around when she could. That would be time enough to get after her. Esau expected it would take a few days. In the meantime he left her to her sorrow, and sent his best hunter to bring back the hide. The man looked forward to tracking the beast and killing it. He had every confidence he could fulfill his master's wish. For one thing, it gave him a chance to stay away from the ranch and be on his own. But there was more. To kill the animal you had to become the animal, a transformation invoked by the hunter. His senses, normally alert, became even sharper when he was out there. His hearing, his sense of smell, his ability to see even out of the corners of his eyes–he was no longer a slave, no longer even human, but a predator, the destroyer, a beast himself.

Journey camped by the stream running through the canyon. She hobbled her horse and fed the paint oats from the palm of her hand, laid out the buffalo robe, and gathered sticks for a fire, but did not light it. She simply wanted to have it ready in case she returned in darkness. When she heard a snort from behind her, she turned to see the colt standing there. Journey whistled and held out a piece of apple; the colt came forward and took it from her hand. She set the bucket of milk in a shallow of the stream, filled the horn with it, and put the teat in the colt's mouth. He sucked on it like it was his mother's. It made Journey feel as if life rushed through her. For an instant, she thought she would float away. Her smile was as wide as the canyon. She laughed, and the young horse snickered back.

The wounds were still terrible, but Journey was relieved to see that they had not festered. She took the salve from her saddlebag and applied it to the gashes, taking the time to be extra cautious when applying it on the one that cut across the horse's eye, because she did not want to get any medicine into it. The colt snickered again and nuzzled her, and when the girl was finished applying the salve she took a brush and began to curry him. She cared for him all day, and when she went for a walk he ambled along beside her. That night the lion took a lamb, and the instant Reuben heard about it he determined to go after Journey.

———— ∞∞∞ ————

She'd been in the canyon two days and two nights. The weather had held. The grass had turned green, and tonight the moon was full. Journey had trapped a fat rabbit in a deadfall. Now it cooked on a spit over the open fire, and grease spattered on the flames. She ate the rabbit with a biscuit followed by an apple and cold, clear water from the stream. Reuben had taught her that the cold water could taste like anything she wanted it to be. That evening she wanted cider, and that's what she got. Journey was happy. She lay back on the buffalo robe covered with her blanket, and looked up at a sky spackled with stars. Her paint could roam with its hobbles but was content to stay nearby, and the colt slept beside her all night.

———— ∞∞∞ ————

Journey's campsite was being watched from another vantage point high up on the canyon wall. The lion lay on a flat ledge under an overhang. In the chalky light of the moon the beast was barely distinguishable from the rock. A snicker reached it. He flicked the black tip of his tail, rubbed his paw over his eyes, stared at the campfire far below: a fallen star. Something above him caught his attention. A hunter. The man stalked the lion from the rim of the canyon wall. The wind shifted, and the hunter stepped cautiously down from the wall, no longer a silhouette. When he reached a granite overhang, he knelt to inspect it closely. He felt the flat rock beneath the overhang with his hand. It was warm. It was silent. He detected a musky odor, smelled his hand, and started to stand. The lion hit him from behind, slammed the hunter's head into a rock. The man was already dead when the cat sank its fangs into the back of his neck.

The next morning Reuben made his way down the ridge and into Wild Horse Canyon. A cluster of vultures croaked in anger, and rose from a clump of pinon some few yards in front of him. Reuben rode over and discovered the carcass of a small horse. Its bones were still sticky and dark brown hair tufted the kill. He found lion tracks and studied them. They were large, but not larger than a man's hand, and he couldn't tell whether or not the right forepaw showed damage. Then his spine began to grow cold, and he spun around in time to see a flash of tawny hide disappear in thick brush. Reuben was certain it had been a lion, but had it been *the* lion? It hadn't attacked him—he was still alive with all his parts. What did that mean? And where was Journey?

Reuben remounted and rode deeper into the canyon. He followed the stream as he knew she would have and finally reached her campsite, her hobbled horse, the buffalo skin and blanket, the ashes of her campfire, but they were cold. Reuben had brought an extra bucket of milk; he put it into the stream next to the one that was nearly empty. Journey's tracks led upstream alongside those of a small horse. It looked like she hadn't been there for a while, but she certainly hadn't broken camp yet, either. She'd be back, so it made sense to sit still and wait. He removed his boots and soaked his feet in the cold water, gnawed on a biscuit and a piece of jerky he had brought, smiled when he thought of Journey's ease with horses, and grinned and flushed with pleasure when he thought what a gift the child was. She and the colt came in at sunset. Journey wondered, from a distance, who had started the campfire, and was pleased when she saw it was Reuben. He was the father she had known, and he was the father she loved without question, as she knew he loved her. He was old, and she did not know what she'd do without him, would rather not have that thought but couldn't keep it far away. She loved Pritta, too, and Joel and Eden, but Pritta stayed at some distance, always seeming to hide behind the patch over the scar where her nose had been, a sadness she couldn't shake. Pritta rarely smiled, while Reuben smiled generously and often. In his heart of hearts, he didn't think smiling became a warrior and a hunter, but also in his heart of hearts he couldn't help it. The child gave him such happiness as he never imagined existed on this earth.

Journey smiled and waved when she recognized him. She raised her hand, which held another rabbit she'd caught when the sun began to go down, and soon it, too, was roasting on a spit, spattering its grease, and giving both of them pleasure at the thought of such a meal. Reuben examined the colt, pleased to see the gashes were healing. Journey had cared for the colt well, although there would be scars where the skin knit together, and Reuben couldn't tell if the scratched eye would lose its sight, or already had. There was no question the colt was damaged, but it seemed not to know it, seemed calm and content in their presence, and pleased to graze close by. When darkness came Reuben wrapped himself in his blanket, and the both of them lay back to stare at the sky. He told her about the stars, where they would take her, how, and when. He told her all things he had told her before, all things she relished hearing again. Reuben fell asleep first, it seemed in the middle of a sentence. She fed the colt milk and a pinch of biscuit, then fell asleep herself.

———∞∞∞———

The two of them—Reuben and Journey—three if you counted the colt, spent a lazy day exploring the canyon. Reuben thought he spotted a cave high up the canyon wall.

"Maybe we'll find gold," Reuben suggested. He didn't really believe it, but you never knew what you were going to find in ancient places. Journey didn't figure they would, but the sheer fancy of it made her tingle with delight.

There was no way to reach the cave on horseback, so they tethered their horses and made the climb. Journey rejoiced that Reuben could still climb like a young man. There was, indeed, a cave, and it offered everything a cave dweller would want: protection from the elements, water and game nearby, protection from their enemies, and a great sweeping vista that looked up and down the entire canyon. The roof was scorched from ancient campfires. There were shards of pottery, the splintered bone fragments of a long ago meal, and even a stone spear point. A hand, now no doubt dead, had drawn a herd of horses on the cave wall with a piece of charcoal—stick figures of the most basic variety, but still they rendered the energy of a running band. Way up canyon, Reuben and Journey could see the herd that was there today.

"Let's run with them," said Journey.

"Let's go," said Reuben.

They reached the canyon floor, drank some water, and mounted up. Journey and Reuben rode towards the herd at a leisurely pace, so as not to spook the wild ones. The colt followed behind them. Had they been on foot they would never have gotten anywhere near the herd. Right now, at this distance, anyway, they were merely more four-legged creatures.

"Where's the stallion?," she wanted to know.

"Shh," cautioned Reuben.

Some time ago, the two of them had been riding up a high mountain trail when Journey saw a cow on the trail ahead. "Somebody's cow got out," she said. At least, she thought it was a cow.

"Shh." Again, Reuben.

It took another step before Journey suddenly realized it wasn't anybody's cow at all; it was an elk. They had ridden right into the middle of an elk herd. The animals were grazing peacefully in an open glade. Journey spotted the bull watching her suspiciously from the wooded edge, a royal bull—seven points! It hadn't completely hit her—what had happened, where they were—when the enormous bull raised his head and bugled, and the herd disappeared like a sand painting when the wind blows, like magic. Not another sound. Fifty huge animals vanished into the woods with no trace at all that they had been there. Journey looked to Reuben. Had he seen what she'd seen? Did it really happen? He smiled and winked.

As they approached the herd the wild horses showed no sign of alarm. The stallion stood on the far side, a dominant, brilliant white. He didn't graze, only watched. A younger stallion, a buckskin, grazed towards him. The instant the buckskin crossed whatever line the white stallion had in mind, the big white spun around and slammed the younger horse in the chest with both rear hooves. The kick would have killed most living things, but not this animal. The buckskin simply shook it off, and returned to his proper place in the herd.

Reuben and Journey reached the herd, and the horses let them in. A handful of fillies surrounded the little chestnut colt, who seemed glad to see them. They bucked and frolicked, nipped and tussled, and ran happily around the perimeter of the herd. Reuben could tell that Journey was inching towards the white stallion, so he warned her off. She whistled loudly for the colt, who whinnied back from a distance. The herd parted and let him through as he galloped towards Journey. This, or something else, alarmed the white stallion. He gave a signal, reared up on his hind legs, and the entire herd responded as one horse. They raced in his direction as he stayed behind to bully lagging horses to keep up with the herd. Journey didn't think she'd ever seen a horse so fast. He circled the herd then, running hard, and resumed his place at its head. There must have been a hundred horses. The chestnut was somewhere in there hidden from view. Both riders were a part of it all: two more horses racing with the herd. Journey felt as if she were one of them, but when she saw Reuben pull back so did she. Their horses had saddles and weren't accustomed to that kind of pace. The two riders stood side by side and watched as the herd disappeared. The young chestnut, somewhere in its midst, disappeared with them.

"That's where he belongs," Reuben told Journey.

Journey knew it, but still she was sad.

They were yet a couple of miles distant up canyon from their campsite when a rifle shot cracked out. Its echo caromed back and forth against the cliffs, but it had come from the vicinity of the camp. They broke into a trot and, as they drew closer, they could see a bunch of men and horses. Only one of the men was white, a big man, bigger than the others: it was Esau Burdock. Of the other four, two were African and two Mexican. They all turned to watch Journey and Reuben ride up. The carcass of a mountain lion hung from the limb of a tree with a rope around its neck. A breeze, not big but insistent, made the lion swing slowly from side to side. At about the same time Journey and Reuben heard hoof beats behind them, the men all shouted and pointed in their direction. Journey turned to see the chestnut colt galloping after them, his flaxen mane and tail flying, all four feet hidden by the dust they kicked up, his white socks making it seem as if he raced on air.

Journey half expected him to stop and nuzzle her for an apple, a piece of biscuit, more milk, but she'd misjudged him. The colt's eyes were bulging and fearsome. Froth flew from his mouth. He'd gone wild and was intent on the lion. He charged past Journey and attacked the dead thing hanging from the tree with a savage rage. The lion swung away, came back, and when its body slapped the colt across the face it made him even wilder. He kicked and bit, and every time the carcass swung back he kicked and bit more ferociously than before.

"Stand back! It's crazy!" Esau bellowed to his men.

They did, but Journey dismounted with her lariat and rushed forward.

"Get away!" shouted Esau

Journey paid no attention. Her focus was the raging colt. She was talking to it, trying to calm it down.

"You're going to get your brains bashed in," hollered Esau. "Back off! Get away!" He turned to Reuben. "Is she crazy? He'll kill her." He ordered one of his men to "Shoot that god-damn thing!" But by now Journey had the loop of the rope around the colt's neck. "No," yelled Journey. "Don't shoot him. Don't shoot!" She pulled the loop tight, spoke to the colt, urging him to back away.

"Cut that lion down and get it out of here!" she yelled at Esau. It had been longer than he remembered was the last time Esau had been given an order, but he took this one with-out thought, and only later did he wonder why.

"You heard what she said. Do it!" he ordered. "All of you. Cut it down and get it out of here!"

By the time they had cut the carcass down and dragged it out of sight, the colt had stopped lunging and was beginning to calm down. Journey stroked him, held him, and spoke to him in soothing tones. He bucked a little, stomped and snorted, but was soon calm and nuzzling the girl's pocket for an apple. Everyone looked at her as if she'd just performed a miracle. One of the Mexicans crossed himself.

"*Madre de Dios*," he mumbled.

"*Madre de Dios*," the other one said.

Esau stood stupefied and stared at her. He tried to make a joke.

"Girl like you ought to be married and havin' kids," he said.

"That ain't a girl like me," she answered, held Esau's eyes 'til she was sure he got it. "That's the wrong lion. Too small."

"How'd you know?" asked Esau.

"I saw him," said Journey.

"The right one killed my hunter," said Esau. "Paws like fryin' pans. Sound like what you saw?" Journey nodded. "Back tracked and took him from behind. Bust his head like a melon."

"Right front part torn away?," she asked. Esau nodded. She then led the colt to the bucket in the stream, where she filled the horn with milk and gave it to the horse to suck. He snickered happily. The men stared dumbstruck.

Esau indicated the colt's wounds. "Lion?" he asked.

"His mother got killed tryin' to save him," answered Journey.

"Who saved him?" asked Esau

"I did," said Journey.

"Might as well shoot it," said Esau. "You went to a lot of trouble for something worthless."

"He's not worthless, and you're not goin' to shoot him!"

"He's not yours, Miss Impudence. The law says I can hang a horse thief, and, far as I'm concerned, you're one, caught in the act." Esau snapped his fingers. "Give me a rope," he ordered without even looking. One of his men stepped forward and handed him a lariat. "Keep a watch on the old man," he ordered the others. Esau's men turned their guns on Reuben.

"Sit," ordered one of the Mexicans.

"No," defied Reuben.

"Shoot him if he moves," said Esau.

Esau fashioned a noose as he spoke.

"You ready to hang for somethin' so useless?"

Journey said nothing. The colt's ears went back. He sensed the threat from Esau. The big man laughed, but it was mirthless.

"Lookit the two of you," he said. "Both of you worthless and both ready to die. Lookit him." He indicated the colt. "Can't breed nothin' with blue eyes and a white blaze 'less you want a blind albino. Can't show him 'cause his scars make him ugly."

"You got scars," said Journey rubbing her neck.

"And don't they make me ugly?" he said, and ran his hands around his neck and over the scars burnt by the rope when Livy tried to hang him so many years ago. Livy. Would he never get her out of his mind? She wasn't nothin' more than a slave, but he treated her like royalty, like some kind of countess, and all the time she wanted him dead. That was the look on her face when she whipped the horses. This girl, called Journey, had a look, too. She stood there and defied him, stood right there and stared him down. Esau wasn't afraid of her, but what he felt didn't make him easy. Livy. She ghosted him. What brought her back? "I admire what you did. I truly do. Makes me feel generous. It truly does. You want that horse?"

She didn't like this man, didn't think he was generous, and didn't trust him a bit. Generous? Esau Burdock? To himself maybe. He owned people. He owned horses. Everybody talked about his house like it was a palace, like they'd been inside, which most hadn't. Well, he didn't own her, and he didn't own Reuben, except here he was like a king who made the law ordering men to hold him at gunpoint, men who obeyed him without question. She had no doubt they would have hung her if he said so.

"Take the guns off my father," she said.

"He ain't your father," said Esau.

"Close enough," said Journey. She wondered at her own audacity. "You afraid of him?" No, Esau thought, I'm not afraid of him. I'm afraid of you. Then, in the instant, he fought that thought and drove it from his mind. It wasn't fear, but there was something eating at him, something making him feel ill at ease.

"Put the guns down," he said to his men, and they obeyed. She had asked him, and he had done so. He admired her gall and wanted to feel equal to it. Why? Was it her beauty, apparent even under ten pounds of dirt after how many days in the canyon? Her green eyes that looked at him like they knew him, maybe even mocked him some? "You want that horse?"

"I do. Yes," she answered.

"Here's my deal: you want that horse you come work for me 'til you work him off."

"What'll I do?"

"Stable work. Muck 'em out. Shoe them. Exercise the stock ain't been rode for a while. Beauty care. Keep 'em lookin' good."

"How long?

"Six months."

"That's a long time."

"Longer than it takes to shoot him. Your choice, Journey." He'd never called her by name before.

"Reuben?" she asked.

"How bad you want him?" he asked in return.

"Six months."

Reuben fixed on Esau. "Good food and a decent bed?"

"I'll treat her like she was my own," answered Esau. "See she's safe," said Reuben. A warning, subtle, but meant."I see a girl can take care of herself," said Esau. "That's the way you raised her, right, amigo?"

"I'm just sayin'," said Reuben."

"You go home and get what you need," said Esau to Journey. "Come first thing tomorrow. You, too, amigo," he told Reuben. "Come by and see the place. Cook keeps hot coffee all day."

———— ∞∞∞ ————

Neither Reuben nor Pritta were much for physical affection, but each of them hugged Journey tightly the next morning before she left.

"Don't worry about me," she told them.

Journey rode out before daybreak with the colt tagging along behind. The pastel light of early morning was smiling kindly over the spread when she arrived. Oak trees lined the road leading to a large hacienda, big, strong ones, at attention, like sentinels. Everywhere were the sounds of a ranch awakening: tweets and cackles, grunts, whinnies, and bleats, barking and lowing. Joel had read her the story of Noah's Ark from *The Bible*, and she thought of it now. Esau was out the door of his hacienda before she tied up. She'd never seen such a grand house in all her life. What could you possibly do with all that room?

"Had breakfast?" he asked.

"Yep," she said.

"Coffee?"

"Two cups."

"Lesson number one," said Esau. "There's a way to talk on my place, and that way is, 'Yes, Sir.' You're workin' here you be like all the rest. No special privileges. Got that?"

"Yessir," she replied.

Esau couldn't put his finger on it, not exactly, but he didn't like the way she said.

"Again," he said.

"Yessir."

"You ever call anybody sir before?"

"No."

"No, sir."

"No, sir."

"Ain't that right, Prospero?" Esau asked this of the slave who had just walked up. Prospero had become Esau's stable master.

"Ain't what right, Suh?" asked Prospero as he removed his straw hat. His head was a splotch of gray hair and scalp.

"None of you wants me one bit mean," explained Esau.

"No, Suh, none of us sure don't," answered Prospero.

"This is Journey," said Esau introducing her. Take her over to the stable and get her started. She's free born, so be careful how you talk to her."

"Yes, Suh. Stable's right down here, Miss," he said taking the reins of her paint and leading the way. Journey followed Prospero, and the colt followed Journey. You could reach the stable easily from the big house. A small corral sat outside one end, itself quite large and cleaner than most any place else she'd ever seen (except for the way Eden kept her cottage, of course), and a large riding ring on the other. Prospero opened the gate and led the paint into the corral. Journey and the colt followed. Prospero immediately closed the gate right after them.

"Close it right away," he told Journey. "You don't they'll take off on you quick as you blink."

Days didn't much linger and went by quickly. "Six months'll be nothin'," she thought. First thing she did mornings was to feed and water the horses. After that she mucked out their stalls, cleaned their hooves, shod whichever needed it, exercised them regularly on a lunge line, and sometimes saddled up and rode them. At the end of each day she'd take her paint for a ride and have the colt, who grew bigger by the minute, follow them around. Journey slept outside on her buffalo hide to be near them, and was told to go to the kitchen for her meals.

Pretty much from her first day the Africans came by to gawk at her. Journey was as light as they were dark, so they wanted to see her close up. The small ones shyly touched her skin with the very tips of their index fingers, then darted away. They'd gotten used to Esau with his red hair and beard, but Journey was a woman, considered by the slaves like some kind of princess from a palace. Soon the little ones came to play with her. She helped them up on the horses and walked them around the ring. Prospero warned her Esau probably wouldn't approve, 'specially if she let her work slip. She liked the little ones so much that she worked extra hard so she couldn't be accused of shirking her duties. If Esau wanted her to stop it, he'd best have good reason. Often at night when she slept she'd awaken to see him watching her, outside the fence, his arms on the top rail. Esau never spoke to her, simply stood there. Journey felt uncomfortable and wished he was someplace else, but then she'd fall back asleep, and come morning he was gone with never a word about it.

Sunday was a day of rest, but only if the slaves attended church, so nearly everyone did, including Esau. It was thought he wanted to set a good example, but really, he was there to see who was present. If a field hand wasn't there, Esau wanted him in the field where he belonged. He also went to make certain the minister had the right attitude. There were known to be abolitionist preachers, mostly up North, but you never could figure what was going to filter down. Esau wanted his preacher to give sermons that called on the Negroes to accept and rejoice in their rightful place on earth, to be obedient and not rebel, to fulfill their duties as God's children, too. The slaves would all occupy the last few rows of the church; the whites all sat up front. Journey attended as well, sitting somewhere in the middle. She did not feel comfortable sitting beside Esau.

Saturday night was the time for dancing. Rejoice! Rejoice! Sunday be a day for rest. Journey heard the singing and the clapping and all the feet tapping, the drum beats and laughter, and took herself down to the slave quarters to watch. Dignified walking, prancing, strutting, and flirting–Saturday night was the time to forget about your labors and just plain old flat out have fun. Journey had never experienced anything like it. Apache dances were all so serious. The dancing of the mountain men was drunk and lurching. But the dancing of the Negroes propelled its participants to ecstasy. Everything moved, every last bit of their bodies, not like the rich white folks who didn't move nothin' from their necks to their hips. Journey was mesmerized and couldn't help moving herself, couldn't help suddenly breaking out in dance with all her whole body while the Africans stood aside, cheering and clapping, beating the drums to keep up with her, drums that took over her very own soul.

Somebody must've told old Esau on her because he came down to the slave quarters hopping mad, grabbed Journey, and hauled her back to the hacienda. That about did it for the dancing that night. Folks just lost the mood. Journey had never seen anybody so angry like Esau was. He squeezed her wrist so tightly it hurt something fierce, all but dragged her off her feet, fuming about you don't dance with the stock, you don't do nothin' with 'em, you hear me? She heard him all right. You don't go down to their quarters nor sit with them nor eat their food nor drink from the same cup. You're a white woman, goddamnit! Act like a goddamn white woman, not no goddamn whore! That Saturday night Esau moved Journey into a bedroom in the hacienda right down the hall from his. Sunday church service he made her sit in the front row right next to him, and starting Sunday evening he had her eat dinner with him at his table. But that same Saturday night Esau couldn't sleep. Before he busted through the circle of slaves that surrounded her he glimpsed her dancing, saw her moving a way he'd never seen a white woman do. He couldn't sleep for thinking about it. Her. Journey. It occurred to Esau that maybe a conjure woman had put the girl in his mind except he could come up with no good reason why the witchwife'd do such a thing.

Journey's new bedroom had been kept as if someone still lived in it, cleaned and dusted, fresh linen, a closet full of dresses. Eden always wore dresses, but Journey had never had a dress on in her entire life, although when she saw the ones in the closet, held them up and looked at herself in the full length mirror, she knew they'd fit. Esau's instructions were to wear one every evening when she sat to dinner. She didn't mind so much wearing one. It was having to eat with Esau that she minded. Before she sat down he had to inspect her, made her turn around and hold the dress out, lift it just a little.

"Moccasins don't go with that," he'd say.

"Yes, Sir," she'd reply, "But moccasins is all I got."

"Then we'll have to get you the proper shoes," he'd say. "We'll take your measure and send away for some."

It wasn't long before the shoes arrived from New Orleans. They were hard on her feet and she much preferred her moccasins.

"When you wear a dress you wear shoes," insisted Esau. "You wear 'em they'll break in soon enough."

———— ∞∞∞ ————

Esau never said so aloud, but he enjoyed having Journey at his dinner table. She ate as much as a man, but the hard work she did daily kept her lithe and strong. He also got pleasure leaning on the fence rail watching while she worked the horses, especially the chestnut colt. His wounds had healed into scars like braided rope. The scratched eye looked blurred over, so Esau was pretty certain he couldn't see out of it. But if you ignored all that, looked at him from the proper angle, the colt was truly a beautiful animal, especially if he was standing in sunlight. He glowed in the sun—his mane and tail reflective of the light— and sometimes he looked like he had a halo all around him.

While Esau enjoyed having Journey at his table, knowing she was in a bedroom down the hall was another matter. He had taken to knocking on her door to say goodnight before he retired to his own room, but he never opened the door, never walked through it even though there was no lock. He fought the urge to do so, telling himself he had no right. She had family close by, such as it was, and she was freeborn. He had no right. Even Esau had a code, such as it was, and Reuben Moon might have been an old man but he was an old man you didn't want to trifle with. Leave the girl alone and get your money's worth out of her, Esau would tell himself. If he wanted a woman, then there were plenty on the ranch to choose from.

Still, Journey appeared in his dreams. He didn't appreciate it, didn't want her there and wished he could banish her from them. It was enough to see her when he was awake. They didn't go to sordid places, his dreams. He'd see her on horseback riding away from him. He'd watch her mount up, swing her right leg over the saddle, and settle into a perfect seat, always, however, with her back to him. Esau never saw her face, but nevertheless knew who it was. The thing was, however, she always wore a dress, never her buckskins, but a dress, a pretty dress, one bought for her, sent away to New Orleans where it had been shipped from Paris, always the latest fashion.

—◦◦◦◦—

Although he hadn't made a kill of late, the lion's tracks were seen all over the ranch—the stables and the corrals, especially, but the pastures, too, and the slave quarters. Esau appointed men to stay awake and watch out for him, including the two slave catchers, Cottonmouth and Meshach. They didn't have anything better to do since nobody had run away recently and they could use the money, so they signed on and got their meals for hanging around, staying sober, and keeping their eyes open. None of this made any difference. The lion would walk behind them and around them, even up close to the big house, but not a soul saw him. It was only a matter of time until another kill.

The night it happened there was no moon out, so it was darker than usual, perfect cover for a beast that could conceal itself in a patch of weeds. The guards and watchmen heard a sudden panic coming from the sheep pen, sheep bleating like they caught on fire. Whatever men were nearby ran over with their guns ready. The sheep were milling around, trying to break out and jumping all over each other, but nobody saw a lion. Right then they heard the cows bawling in the pasture and ran over. By the time the men got there the lion had taken a calf and disappeared. They could see where he went under the fence, and they could see where he went over the fence, but what nobody could see was him. Two days later, the lion took a little girl on her way back from the outhouse. Two days after that, on a hot night when the doors and windows were left open, the lion entered a cabin and took a sleeping baby from his bed. Esau was losing money. That's when he placed a bounty of three thousand dollars on the lion's hide.

Some weeks after Esau Burdock pulled Journey away from the dance, Eunice, one of his slaves, came home from the fields one day to find her son, six-year-old Socrates, playing in the dirt with stones in front of their cabin. He was making them into a tower, shooting them like marbles, just little six-year-old play stuff. A glint of fading sunlight caused her to look twice at what he was doing. She rushed over to him and said,

"Lemme see dat."

"What?" he asked clenching something tightly in his little fist. She slapped his hand.

"Right now, boy. Lemme see dat."

He began to whimper, but obeyed his mother and opened his fist for her to see.

"Where you get dat?" she demanded.

"I found it," he whimpered.

"You stole it!" she accused, taking it from him.

"No, ma'am, I swear I found it," he protested.

"Where?" she wanted to know, "Somebody's drawer you ain't s'posed to be into?"

"I found it. I swear."

What Socrates had was a little green stone a gold chain carved like a fat-bellied, smiling man sitting cross-legged with two fingers in the air.

"Tell me quick, or I'll whup you good," she threatened. He was terrified now.

"She dropped it!"

"Who dropped it?"

"The white woman. At the dance. I found it in the dirt after she gone. I swear, Momma, I din't steal it!

"You din't give it back neither, did you?"

"No, ma'am. I was goin' to, but. . . "

"But, what?" The little boy could think of nothing more to say.

"Dat's stealin' then. Same thing as stealin'. Mastuh Burdock know you got dat he'll whup your hind parts harder den I ever could."

"Don't whup me, momma. I din't mean no wrong."

Eunice loved this child beyond imagining, so much she wish she could cut off her hand rather than hurt him with it. But she knew Mastuh Esau'd hurt him more, beat her little boy 'til the man's arm was tired then beat him with the other, do all that if he caught him stealing. It would be just worse than she'd ever do, so she smacked him hard and smacked him again, then sent him to bed without supper. That night she took the necklace and went up to the hacienda to see the master.

When Eunice knocked and was allowed in, Esau was sitting in his library nursing a brandy and enjoying a fine cigar. He was looking to see how long the ash could get before it broke off. Esau had learned to read when he was a slave trader back in New Orleans, and his library was well stocked for the time and place. Of course, he had a *Bible*, both Old and New Testaments, an atlas of the known world, sermons by noted ecclesiasts, texts on animal husbandry, the complete works of William Shakespeare, Aristotle, Plato, and a Latin version of Caesar's Gallic wars, all these leather bound by a fine hand and most imported from England. Esau didn't read Latin, and he barely read the others, just picked and poked at random, but it was his conviction that an educated man of means ought to have a well-stocked library, and it was his desire to be thought an educated man, albeit an autodidact, a word he was extraordinarily proud to have in his vocabulary. He thought it a shame there were not many occasions to use it. His latest acquisition was by a writer who was all the rage on both continents, Washington Irving, and Esau was reading about the Headless Horseman when Eunice knocked. This was a ghost he could understand, not that bellyacher who was Hamlet's father.

Eunice entered the library, curtsied, bowed, shifted foot to foot, barely able to speak. She was in the presence of the single person who controlled every aspect of her being. He could work her day and night, limit her rations, whip her, sell her, worse, sell her son so she'd never see the boy again. Rather he should whip the boy instead. At least, she'd still have him.

"Tell me who you are and why you're here," Esau said kindly. He thought of himself as a fair and just master, although stern like the Old Testament prophets.

"Name's Eunice, Suh," she stammered. She was terrified before her master. She'd never spoken a word to him before. She wanted to drop down on her knees and beg him to whip her boy, not sell him. How to talk? What to say? Don't say nothin' 'bout Socrates. Leave the boy out.

"Speak up, girl," said Esau, not gruffly.

"Eunice, Suh."

"Eunice," he said. "Don't you have a little boy to put to bed about now?"

How'd the mastuh know dat?

"Go on. Speak up. What is it?" he asked.

She could say nothing, so she simply stepped forward and held out an open hand. The necklace on its gold chain. The green stone, the cross-legged fat man, the one smiling. Esau took it and held it up, and, as he realized what it was, a wail erupted from deep inside him as if a knife had been shoved into his heart. Eunice expected rage, though not this, but seeing her master this way scared her even more. He fell back in his chair. His face blanched. He struggled for words, and had only a rattle in his throat that sounded like death. He seemed to have been suddenly drained of strength.

"Where?" Esau could barely get the word out.

"Suh?" asked Eunice

"Where did this come from?"

"Found it, Suh."

"Where?"

"In the dirt, Suh."

"Did you steal it?"

"Oh, no, Mastuh Esau. No. I swear," she said.

"Where did this come from?" he demanded.

"It fell off her when she dance," explained Eunice.

"Who?" he asked.

"Miss Journey. It fell off her in the dirt and she din't know."

Another wail escaped him, sounded like, "Oh wo oooh oh . . ." An awful wail.

"The dance was weeks ago. Why'd you wait so long?"

"Please don't beat him, Suh! Please don't sell him away!"

"What are you talking about?" Esau wanted an answer.

"My little boy, Suh. He found it and been playin' with it. Didn't mean nothin', Suh. Soon's I saw it I slapped him good."

"Go away, Eunice."

"Suh?"

"Go away, Eunice!"

She ran from the library, never so glad to be shut of a place in her life.

Esau knew. He knew! But what was it he knew? He could not grasp. . . what? what?. . . how this could be? It stunned him. He did not move for fear his heart would give out and pitch him to the floor. The dead. The dead. The dead had returned to torture him, to haunt him, to drive her nails once more into his flesh and soul. Every fiber of him strained for mercy. *Oh, God. Oh, God. Do not do this to me again!*

Journey hadn't yet undressed for bed. She stood with her back to the door before the full-length mirror with a dress held up in front of her. It was a pleasant surprise that she enjoyed dresses as much as she did. She certainly didn't want to wear them all the time or even most of the time, but now and then, yes, it was fun and made her more than she had known she was. "There are surprises in this world," she thought to herself.

The bedroom door opened behind her and Esau stood there staring at her. She turned around and looked at him full on, and he cried out, "Livy! Livy!" The woman in his dream. The woman on horseback riding away from him. She turned around and it was Livy. She was Livy. Journey didn't understand. Who was Livy? Why had he called her that? Ruddy every time she had seen him, his face was now bloodless. His breath seemed to have stopped. He stood there and held out the necklace in his hand.

"Oh," she said, "I thought it was lost. Thank you." Journey was so happy to see it again. "Where did you find it?"

"Where did you get it?"

"I've always had it. It belonged to my mother."

"Girl, do you know what you're saying?"

"Reuben gave it to me. It was my mother's, only she was dead at my birth."

The entire weight of this came crashing in on him.

"What's wrong?" she asked.

"Do you know who you are?"

"Who am I?"

"You are mine!"

"What?"

"Mine. Mine!"

Suddenly, he sounded so angry. Now she was frightened. His countenance had darkened. His breathing quickened. He snatched the dress from her hand, threw it on the floor, threw her on the bed, and fell on her like a starving bear. His was an awful weight. He pressed on her, and she could not breathe. He tore at her clothing. She could only think to get away. He tore the bodice of her dress. Journey grabbed the oil lamp from her bedside table and smashed it against Esau's head. His hair caught fire. His face. He screamed as the burning oil fell on the bed. She lurched aside, lunged away, and ran out the door.

House slaves were running down the hall to her room. Someone yelled, "Get water! Get water!" Nobody paid attention to Journey as she ran in the opposite direction, down the stairs, into the kitchen, from there out the back door, hugging the shadows. But Glorybee stood there blocking the back door, stood there resolute with a kitchen knife in her hand. Journey lurched to a stop, grabbed the table to keep from falling. No way to get around that woman. "Come on," indicated Glorybee, and stepped aside as Journey bolted past her and out the door. She was thinking, Journey was, thinking, "Stay hid. Keep low. Reuben. I need Reuben." She knew she had to get out of there, run, keep running, stay low, keep hid. Journey made her way from behind the house and behind the stable to where she could see the corral. If she could get to her horse. . . But the two slave catchers were at the gate. She couldn't. She had to run. She took to the woods. A few steps in, she sensed someone behind her and lurched away as a hand clamped over her mouth. It was Prospero. He put two fingers to his lips and handed Journey a battered old canteen full of water. She took it and headed home.

One side of Esau's face was burned and half the hair on his head, but he had clasped a pillow to his face and smothered the flames. He ran from the room bellowing, "Livy! Livy! I want her back! Get her back!," while his slaves extinguished the rest of the fire. It hardly mattered. The bedroom was ruined.

Journey kept to the woods beside the dirt road to hide her tracks, though she knew it wouldn't be long before the slave catchers were onto her. The fact that it was a dark night with a slip of a moon and no stars slowed her down, but she made it to Joel's and Eden's cabin by dawn. The coffee was on, meaning that they were already up tending the stock and generally getting about their day. Reuben was stoking the forge with the intent of making horseshoes that morning. Pritta had gone up river to set fish traps. Journey was dirty and scratched from her escape, and her dress was even more tattered than when she ran from Esau. Joel and Eden had by no means expected her and called out, "Journey, Journey." Obviously, there was something wrong, but she ran by them calling for Reuben and threw herself against him, clutching him to her, hanging on, something she'd never done before.

"Who is Livy?" she cried. Reuben had never heard the name before. "He said he owned me."

"Who?" asked Reuben.

"Esau. He said I was his. He kept screaming, 'Mine! Mine!'"

Eden came over with a shawl to protect Journey against the morning chill. Joel brought her coffee, but her hands were shaking too much to hold the cup. Reuben knew he'd better hide her good because the slave catchers would be after her soon, probably were already.

"Why did he say that, Reuben?" insisted Journey. Reuben knew why, but it was as if he had lockjaw and couldn't speak.

"What happened, child?" asked Eden.

"I lost my necklace, and he found it. He was crazy, broke into my room yelling, 'Livy! Livy!' He threw me on my bed, but I smashed the oil lamp against his head and got away."

Reuben had his answer. He had forgotten about the necklace, taken from around her own neck and given to him by Journey's mother before she died. The child always wore it inside her clothes, yes, but how could he have forgotten? Esau would know. He did know. It belonged to Journey's mother, who must have gotten it from Esau. Livy was her grandmother. Livy. What had happened to her?

"It was your mother's. She got it from her mother and asked me to give it to you before she died. Her name was Lilly Rose. Her mother's name must've been Livy. Esau owned them," said Reuben.

The meaning of all this stunned everyone standing there.

"He owns me?" she cried.

"Nobody owns you, child," said Joel.

"He owns me?" she cried out again. "He's my father? He's my grandfather?"

The old man's agony was such that he could have flayed the skin from his own body, but there was no time to indulge how he felt. He had to get her hidden, and then he had to get her someplace else. Mexico. They'd go to Mexico, though he knew the slave catchers would try to trace them there. He would not let her leave his side. He would protect her.

"Let's get you hidden," he said. He knew those men would scour his cabin and this place. They were lethal and they would be thorough, especially if Esau had put a price on her head, a bounty, like a hunted animal, which Reuben was sure he had.

"Let's get you hidden," he said. "You people act like nothin' happened," he told Joel and Eden. They'd both need to be good actors like in a play. "You ain't seen her," he told them. "Get about your business." With that he took Journey some way into the woods and built a bower low to the ground of sticks and branches, bade her crawl into it, and covered it with a downed tree. As long as she stayed in it she'd be invisible. Reuben was satisfied she'd stay hidden. He'd never seen those men with dogs and hoped to God they wouldn't come, but knew they would. Where else could Journey have gone? Journey. Journey. His Journey and now Esau's? God wouldn't be so cruel. But, He already had.

———— ∞∞∞ ————

The slave catchers came as Reuben knew they would. He was working at the forge when they arrived. Joel was working in his carpentry shop. Eden appeared on the front porch and offered them coffee, which they bolted down and swallowed hot.

"Thanks for your kindness," said Meshach. "I hope that means you're goin' to make this easy. We're here on legal business. You got a runaway slave here, and we was obliged to get her back. Where is she?"

"We haven't seen her," said Joel.

"How'd you know it was a her?" asked Meshach.

"Search the place," said Eden.

"My guess is that'd be a waste of time," said Meshach.

"Let's make this easy," said Cottonmouth as he dismounted. "If they run, shoot 'em."

The slave catcher called Cottonmouth took a length of rope, cut it into three pieces, and tied everyone's hands behind their backs. Meshach watched while his partner fastened a noose from another rope and threw the end over the branch of a tree out front the cottage.

"Now," said Meshach, "We expect she's around here somewhere. That gives us options. We could rape your woman while you watch," he said to Joel. "Take her every whichaway. That'd be fun. Or we could hold your man's feet to that fire over there," he said to Eden, referring to the forge. "Or we could hang him." He meant Reuben. "I'm not so sure that'd force you to tell, but let's see."

Cottonmouth pushed Reuben over to the tree and placed the noose around his neck.

"You can't do this," yelled Joel.

"You offerin' us your wife?" asked Meshach.

"What kind of men are you?" she asked.

"The kind standin' right here in front of you. Give us a job, and we do it. You folks're harborin' a runaway, and that's against the law. We know what you're doin', and we're goin' to find her. Stretch him out," he said to Cottonmouth, and Cottonmouth pulled the rope tight, not so tight as to cut off Reuben's breath, but tight enough to feel it.

"You can't do this!" screamed Eden.

"Looks like we are though, don't it?" replied Meshach.

"He's an old man," she screamed.

"You sayin' he's lived long enough?" asked Meshach. To Cottonmouth, "Pull it tighter." He did. He pulled it tight enough to stretch out Reuben's neck but keep his feet on the ground. Reuben began to strangle. The old man fought to breathe. "They told me you breeds were tough. Now I see for myself. You want to tell me where she is?"

Reuben couldn't speak, could only gag. He jerked his head from side to side. "That a no?" asked Meshach. "Anybody else?" he asked looking at Joel and Eden. Again, Reuben jerked his head from side to side. "Tighter," Meshach said. Cottonmouth obeyed. Reuben gagged and came up on tiptoe, his feet less than a shade off the ground. "Journey," hollered Meshach, "Come on out before we hang the old man!" To Cottonmouth, "Tighter." Cottonmouth leaned on the rope and Reuben's feet came up off the ground. Now, Reuben could not breathe. He dangled and jerked at the end of the rope.

"Stop it," screamed Eden, "Stop it!"

"Hey, Journey, you best get out here before he dies," shouted Meshach. To Cottonmouth, "Let 'im down." Cottonmouth eased up on the rope so Reuben's toes are once again touching the ground. "You goin' to tell me where she is?" asked Meshach. Reuben gagged and jerked his head from side to side. "Take 'im up," ordered Meshach. Reuben's feet came up off the ground. Again, he dangled and jerked

"You're animals!" screamed Eden.

"The good Lord's creatures," said Meshach. Cottonmouth laughed and pulled Reuben up a little higher. The old man's eyes bulged. His face turned blue. "You got about a minute to get out here, girl!" he bellowed.

"She's not here, for God's sake," yelled Joel.

"You're next, son," said Meshach.

She couldn't stand it anymore. Journey fought her way through the branches and charged Cottonmouth. He let Reuben drop to the ground, pulled his knife and turned on her. "Mr. Burdock wants you alive, but he'll take you any way he can," he said. The man was actually smiling. Journey held herself back. She had nothing to fight him with.

"Guess you were right, Meshach," Cottonmouth said to his partner.

Meshach tossed a set of manacles at her feet. Cottonmouth locked them on her on her wrists. He took the noose from around Reuben's neck and put it around Journey's. He held onto the free end and mounted up. "Much obliged," said Meshach. Cottonmouth tipped his hat and touched heels to his horse. The slave catchers rode away with Journey, the rope around her neck, walking behind them.

———— ∞ ————

Book 3

MESHACH NEVER LOOKED BACK AT ALL. HE KEPT SLUGGING from a jug of hard cider and was well into one of his periodic drunks before they were half way to Burdock's. On the other hand, Cottonmouth couldn't help but look back. He had a fish on the line, oh, yes, he did, and what a beauty she was! Yellow hair. Near white. Green eyes. Skin like milkweed. Damn! Untouched he guessed, unless maybe Esau'd done her. Or the old Indian. Mexican. Whatever he was. Or the one was a doctor. Maybe the woman. He'd heard about that. Cottonmouth would look back, lick his lips, and make kissing sounds. He'd flick his end of the rope and watch its ripples float their way back to her neck, just to annoy her. But he wanted to do more than annoy her. If she was his he'd sure show her somethin'.

Journey had on no petticoats, so he could see her shape under the material of her dress. Cottonmouth couldn't remember the last time he had a white woman, couldn't remember because, goddamnit, he never had, only coloreds, Mexicans, and Indians. He wondered, "Could he get away with it?" Tell

Meshach to stop here just a minute, lay the girl flat, even take the manacles off, just go at her from behind. But, she'd tell Esau, wouldn't she? Probably, she would. And Esau would believe her. Probably, he would. And if she told him and if he believed her Cottonmouth would no doubt die a painful death, maybe even Esau would boil him in a cauldron. He knowed of slaves done like that before, seen it once himself, seen slaves hung from a gibbet and cut in half, seen them beat to death and skinned alive, none of which did Cottonmouth desire for his own self. Didn't desire none of that but did desire her. He turned around and rode backward in the saddle, looked at her, licked his lips and made kissing sounds as he relieved himself. Oh, yeah, she was a pretty somethin'! Where'd she get that name? Journey.

She shut her eyes tight so she wouldn't have to see him. He was filthy, and when the wind shifted she caught his smell, an odor so vile it caused her to gag. What was happening to her? Journey had never known anything but freedom and people who loved her, only now she'd reached the point where the filth in front of her could hang an old man from a tree and be right to do it. Esau Burdock made it be. His word. His law. She'd die before he had his way, but she knew enough to know that a man like him could cause so much pain and agony a person would do anything. Journey had never felt fear before, but she felt it now. She wanted to be strong, to walk tall and defy him in front of everyone, but fear made her reel, and shake, and dwell on the awful. She had never known what made people turn and run but she felt it now, insides strangled and twisted so you screamed and heard yourself screaming and saw nothing and felt nothing but a sheet of white lightning. She knew she would be punished, but why? Because he said so? He would say she tried to kill him and that was why she needed to be punished. But it wasn't. She knew that. He could say she was to be punished and then punish her good just because he was Esau Burdock. People obeyed him like he was a king in Europe and that's what people did. Because he said so. He took what he wanted because he could. "Oh God, oh God, what is happening to me?"

———— ∞∞∞ ————

Meshach, Cottonmouth, and Journey reached the ranch somewhat before dusk, while people were still at work. Those who could see them stopped and stared. Meshach was so drunk he could barely stay in the saddle, but he had done the job he was sent to do, and here she was, so Esau didn't look at him twice. He came out of the house when they rode up. Journey saw that one side of his face had been badly burned and was covered with a salve, and that half of the hair on his head was gone. His scalp was burned, too, and scarlet patches of it had salve on them as well. Journey had never thought of him as a man of good looks, but now when she looked at him—the burns on his face and scalp, hair gone, what was left singed—he looked half like a beast. He came directly over and asked Cottonmouth did he touch her? When the slave catcher said no, Esau walked over to Journey and asked did he touch you, and that's what she said, too. No. Esau stared at her with an expression she'd never seen before—pain and fury mixed, staring hard as if confused, trying to find something that might not be there—then he backhanded her across the face so hard it was a wonder to those watching that her head didn't fly off.

"Put her in the stable," he ordered. As they walked away, Esau hollered to an overseer to see that all the slaves and everybody else who worked the ranch turned out at dawn to see the girl whipped.

———— ⌾⌾⌾ ————

That night Esau Burdock lay in bed staring at the ceiling, unable to sleep except in fits and starts. Indigestion burned his gullet, and an entire bottle of port did nothing to erase his pain. When he fell asleep, Livy would wake him up. She was still in his dreams, although he did not want her there. He'd see her from behind with her dress pulled down around her hips, see her unblemished alabaster back that tapered gracefully from her shoulders to her waist, her blonde hair piled atop her head, her elegant neck. In his dream her head with the golden ringlets left her body, rose up into the sky and became the moon. The one time he'd beaten her—what was it even for? He could no longer remember—the one time he'd beaten her he'd been careful to use only a leather belt, not a whip, because he did not want to scar her perfect back. He'd hear her laughing and expect her to turn and smile when she saw him. Instead, she looked at him with hatred, Medusa the Gorgon, hair of snakes, eyes that turned a man into stone. Esau had never told anyone of his feelings for Livy, not even Livy. Although she started out as a fancy, a whim of the moment, a rescue, really, he'd come to care for her a great deal. She liked to sing a popular tune when she made his dinner, and she sat by patiently as he talked to her about whatever he fancied, his long trip from the rude streets of London to the elegant parlors of New Orleans, his choice: hang or enter servitude himself, his plans for the future.

One day an elderly sailor had come into the market looking to buy a housekeeper. The man's days at sea were coming to an end, so he had need of a woman to cook and launder, keep his place clean. Esau found one that the seaman deemed suitable, though her price was steep. The sailor had brought a valuable necklace back from a voyage to Japan, and he offered it in trade. The old man explained it was a small Buddha, an Oriental god carved from jade on a true gold chain. It was considered very lucky in the East. Esau thought it perfect for Livy and made the trade. It matched the green of her eyes. He fastened it around her neck, and she never took it off until Lilly Rose was born. Then she gave it to her baby, tied a knot in the chain to shorten it, and placed it around the infant's neck. Lilly Rose really never knew her mother—Livy was executed when the child was still near an infant—but she wore the Buddha always and never took it off. It was right that it had come to Journey, but it was a mystery to Esau how that had happened. How had she come to Reuben Moon? Esau could charge him with harboring an escaped slave and force him to tell. Journey wasn't yet born when Lilly Rose ran away. Esau arose from his bed, dressed, and took the Buddha necklace with him along with a bottle of port as he made his way out of the house down to the stable, where Journey was bound and awaiting punishment. He picked up a small stool before he entered her stall, sat down opposite her while she sat on the hay, opened the bottle of port, and offered her the first drink.

"I didn't think colored was to drink out of the same bottle with white people." Her intent was sarcasm.

"You're my daughter," he said.

"You're my master," she countered.

"Your father."

"No father to me," she replied.

"That breed ain't your father," said Esau.

"I say so," said Journey.

"Don't matter what you say."

"Matters to me."

Esau offered her the bottle. She shook her head.

"I don't want to kill the pain of what you're goin' to do," she said, "Or what you already done. I don't want to do anything but hate you in my heart and blood like a beast."

"If I give you one hundred lashes you won't live," he said.

"Then I won't live, and you won't own me," she said. "If that's what you want you'll get it."

"Your grandmother had a back clear as a marble goddess. The one time I whipped her I didn't leave a mark. Used my belt, not a whip."

"And you expect me to feel what?"

"I don't want to hurt you."

"But you're goin' to."

"I have to. Everybody knows what you did. Stock won't respect me if I don't. They'll slow down, won't work, won't do what I tell 'em, sass me back. I can't have that." He was trying to explain.

"I'm s'pose to feel sorry for you?" she asked.

"I can make it easier on you. I want you to understand."

"I'm a coon, a jig, a gutter monkey. Why would you expect a shitskin like me to understand? Father."

"Don't make this harder than it need be," he warned.

"It's not in my hands. I've got manacles on. Can't even scratch my head. You're the law. You're the rules. I come from the mud. Mud people, ain't that what you call us? Mud people ain't got no souls. Only whites got souls. Rest of us is dredged up out the mud. You stuck your pecker in the mud, and look what you got! What I've got to do with makin' it hard or easy?"

Esau offered her the bottle.

"You want this?" he asked.

"No, damn you, *father,* I do not! Drink the bottle. Make yourself feel good then whip me 'til I die."

"When I was about your age back in England I was offered a choice: hang or be indentured. Same thing as a slave. I chose to be a slave. Didn't look forward to it. Didn't like it. But it turned out to be an opportunity. Changed my life. Gave me a trade. Back in England where a man is born is all the where he's goin' to get forever and eternal. Work hard. Take it easy. Same thing. You're goin' nowhere. I came to this country as nothin' and rose up by my own bootstraps to where I am right now. A man envied by other men. Nobody did it for me. Saw the opportunity and worked hard. Learned to read. Learned to do business. Saved what little money I got a hold of and made it multiply. I was gettin' by and I had hope, but one day I got a dream, too, and that made the difference. I dreamed of raising horses the envy of every man in the world, dreamed of my own herd, dreamed of dressing Livy like a fairytale princess, fine linen and sweet satin, food like the royalty of Europe, folks lookin' up to me, Esau Burdock, a man of means, good fortune, and good sense. I wanted them to point me out when I rode by: 'There he goes, Esau Burdock. He wasn't even born here and look what he done. Son, do your diligence and grow up to be a man just like him.'"

"Tell me more about my grandmother," asked Journey

"You're her," he said, "Tall, fair, green eyes. Hair."

"Like mine?"

"Not as bright."

"When did she die?"

"Your mother was an infant."

"Why did she?"

Esau thought to himself, "What if I told her she tried to hang me?" He felt, as he did every time he thought of it, a mix of bewilderment and pain. Esau forgot for a moment where he was.

"Why did she?" repeated Journey.

"She took sick."

"With what?"

"A disease that Africans get. Some Latin name. I don't remember."

"No cure?"

Esau thought, *The cure was they shot her and put her head on a pike.* Instead he said:

"No."

"What about my mother?" asked Journey.

"Green eyes. All of you."

"What else?"

"Skin like honey."

"Hair?"

"Dark, but soft not stiff. Some red in it."

"My age."

"About."

"What happened to her?"

"She disappeared. Nobody knows."

"Reuben."

"Maybe he'll tell us."

"You'll see him again."

"I expect so."

"You hurt me, you will."

"I guess I will then."

"He'll come and rescue me."

"Last I heard he was all bound up with nobody to untie him."

"Pritta had to come back some time."

"She the one without a nose? That's Apache for you."

"Reuben'll come. I would not want to be you when he does."

"Let's talk about you. It'll be dawn soon, and everybody's goin' to fall out here to see you whipped. It'll be a lesson to them. 'If the mastuh does this to her, what'll mastuh do to me?' They'll see me tear your dress off your back, see your skin all white and pure and watch while the whip shreds it to raw meat. Livy's was that way: white and pure. Tear you up, girl. It's got nine leather braids that whip. Each got a knot at the tip. You never felt such pain."

"Reuben . . . "

"You can hope for that, or you can do what I say."

"I'd rather die."

"Thing is, Journey, you won't die. That's the worst of it. You'll carry that beatin' for the rest of your life.

"I'll kill myself."

"You'll die with the scars."

"I won't bow down to you."

"You're young. Don't have good sense. Hear me out."

"I won't bow down!"

Infuriated, Esau punched Journey in the face so hard he knocked her back.

"Don't be so goddamn stubborn! You're a fool. You're a fool. Don't make me hurt you more'n I need to!" He took a breath, calmed himself down, and continued. Outside the stable door the sky was getting lighter. "It's almost time. All of 'em goin' to be here soon to see justice meted out. When they're gathered I'll bring you outside. You will tell everybody in a loud voice how sorry you are, how you regret your rash actions. You'll call me Father and ask my forgiveness, say you will respect my wishes from this day on. Obey me and I'll let you off easy: fifteen lashes with my belt. No scars. No blood. Redness gone after a day."

"I won't do it," she replied softly, knowing to expect worse.

"Then you'll get twenty lashes with the cat."

"Lord," she said as if it were a gasp. Esau was satisfied Journey had gotten his message.

"Your soul may belong to Jesus, child, but you belong to me."

An overseer stuck his head inside the stable door. He, too, was a slave, black as pitch, but he lorded it over all the rest. "Most of 'em be out there now, boss," he said to Esau.

"Tell me when they're all formed up," said Esau. "I want them in close."

"Yessuh," replied the overseer.

"And send William in here," said Esau.

"Yessuh."

Esau took a swallow of port and held it out to Journey who still refused.

"You think it over," he said.

"Reuben, Reuben," she said softly, but with despair.

"Better say 'Esau, Esau'. I'm your hope now."

A slave named William, a skinny Negro in his twenties, appeared at the door.

"Massuh?" he said.

"Come in here," ordered Esau.

"Yessuh," replied William.

"Turn around and take off your shirt," said Esau. "Let her see your back."

William did as he was told. His back was a mass of thickly braided scars: ropes and ridges, twisted discolored skin. It was gruesome. Journey shuddered and looked away.

"That's all," said Esau.

"Yessuh," bowed the man, put on his shirt, and left the barn.

"You don't have much time, girl," said Esau.

"You don't have to do this," she said softly.

"I didn't hear you."

Journey knew there was nothing she could do to change the man's mind, nothing she would do. How did any man have the right to flay the skin from another's body? Joel had a God he talked to every day. Time to time Joel'd said he got an answer. Journey had never been able to call on Him, so why expect He'd be here now?

"I didn't hear you," repeated Esau.

She shook her head. There was no point.

The overseer appeared in the doorway.

"Mastuh Esau, suh," he said.

Esau looked up as if he were exhausted from carrying the weight of the world by himself.

"You ready?" he asked the man.

"They waitin'," said the overseer.

Esau took Journey under the arm and pulled her to her feet.

"Let's go," he said.

Outside the stable the slaves—it seemed like a hundred of them—were formed up in no special way opposite the corral. Esau led Journey to the corral and turned her around to face the multitude. The horses, Journey's paint and the young colt, whinnied happily and came to the fence as if expecting her to give them a treat. Meshach, still drunk, stood to one side stoking a small fire in which he was heating a branding iron to a red glow. Journey knew what that meant and tried to pull away but Esau snatched her back. Branded by him? Carry Esau's brand for the rest of her life? Inside she was screaming, "Don't show it! Don't show it! You be brave!" She knew the brand: **EB**. She'd seen it on the others. She gasped, "Reuben."

"You see him here?" asked Esau with a smirk, knowing he wasn't.

Cottonmouth stood not far from Meshach and winked at Journey when she looked at him.

"You can say your piece now," said Esau. "Say what I want and get my belt."

"You goin' to burn that into me no matter what I say?" said Journey referring to the branding iron.

"I own you, girl!" said with the exasperation of having to say it again. "I'll own you 'til you falter and die."

"Get it over with," said Journey.

"Bind her to the top rail," he ordered Cottonmouth. The man turned her around roughly, spread her arms along the top rail, and tied her wrists to it, pressing himself against her before he backed away. The colt approached Journey and gently nuzzled her.

"Thank you, boy," she said.

The overseer handed Esau the cat o'nine tails, and Esau held it above his head for all to see.

"Twenty lashes!" he bellowed shaking the whip first to his right then to his left. "Twenty lashes! She's no better than the rest of you!" With that he tore Journey's dress down to her hips. The crowd murmured and some began to cry. They'd never seen such a pure skin as the girl had on her back. Instantly, they knew.

Esau drew back his arm and laid the first blow across her back. That single blow obliterated any thought Journey ever had and replaced it with excruciating pain. Nothing she'd ever felt came close to this, not even the time she burned her hand in a fire.

"One," counted Cottonmouth

Esau lashed her again. Flesh ripped. Blood appeared. Her legs lost their power to hold her up, but the ropes on her wrists kept her in place.

"Two," counted Cottonmouth.

Esau lashed her again. She heard herself cry out. The young colt charged the fence and tried to break through.

"Three."

The moans from the multitude of slaves gathered there to watch grew louder as if the blows were theirs as well.

"Lord, Lord," they cried. "Have mercy, mastuh!"

"Four."

"Have mercy!"

"Five."

What a din the slaves made! How they cried and moaned and screamed for mercy. The young horse screamed, too. He snaked his head over the fence and tried to bite Esau. He slammed the butt of his whip across the horse's nose.

"Back off!"

"Six."

Was no mercy here, no mercy to be given, no mercy to be gotten.

"Seven."

Some of the slaves dropped to their knees and prayed.

"Eight."

Journey wished for death.

"Nine."

Her body had no strength but still it wouldn't die.

"Ten."

Only ten, and her back was already raw meat. The overseers ordered the slaves to be quiet. Moans became muffled but they couldn't stop. Tears ran down their faces. Tears tore from Glorybee's eyes as the old woman stood by helplessly. The young colt fought the fence but couldn't break through.

"Shet your mouths, damn you," ordered the overseers.

"Eleven."

"Shet your damn mouths, you black bastards, or you be next!"

"Twelve"

Journey's back looked like something the dogs chewed on.

"Thirteen."

The lash nicked her neck and blood spurted forth.

"Fourteen."

How many more? How many more? The young horse raced back and forth.

"Fifteen."

"Have mercy!"

An overseer lashed out at the woman who said it.

"I done tol' you. Shet it!"

"Sixteen."

Esau's arm was tired. Only four more.

"Seventeen."

Journey was still conscious. Terrible pain. Not beyond it.

"Eighteen."

Not beyond it.

"Nineteen."

With what strength she had left Journey called for, "Reuben! Reuben!"

"Twenty."

"Now brand her," Esau ordered Meshach.

Journey understood and tried to wrest away, but her struggle was feeble, no more than a twitch. Meshach took the branding iron from the fire and lurched forward drunkenly. In the instant came the sharp crack of a rifle, and his head exploded like a jug of whiskey. He fell to the ground still clutching the branding iron. The crowd looked back and saw a man on horseback racing down the road.

Reuben.

"Shoot that bastard," Esau hollered to Cottonmouth

Reuben re-sheathed his rifle and charged. A wagon driven by Joel, carrying Eden on the seat beside him, appeared and rattled towards them while the gathering stared open mouthed and wide eyed. This was no apparition. This was the Lord coming to take revenge. Cottonmouth missed his shot and Reuben bore down upon him, his lance level to the ground. Instead of panicking, Cottonmouth faced Reuben head on, beat his chest, and brayed like a banshee. Reuben kept on as the lance punched through the slave catcher's chest and left his heart quivering on its shaft. Reuben dismounted, pulled the lance loose, and turned on Esau. With the point of the lance at Esau's neck, the overseers froze in place.

"Cut her loose!" yelled Reuben.

One of the overseers took out his knife to do as Reuben ordered when the wagon reached them and came to a stop. Joel and Eden jumped out and ran to Journey.

"You ain't near human. Pray I kill you quick." said Reuben and forced the lance just enough to pierce the skin of Esau's neck. Reuben couldn't look at Journey's back because he knew he'd kill Esau if he did. Killing the slave catchers was one thing. They were low lifes. Esau was a man of property. You could hang for that.

"Get them back to work." Esau ordered his overseer, his voice and manner undaunted by the lance. If he died he was going to die standing up. The overseer signaled the others and cries of "Back to work!" rang out. Some of the slaves were still crying, but they all turned as one at the order. A woman, somewhere in the multitude, began to sing, low and mournful.

"I looked over Jordan and what did I see?"

Another woman, somewhere else, picked it up and sang, "Comin' for to carry me home."

And another, "A band of angels comin' after me. . . "

And another, "Comin' for to carry me home."

By now, the multitude of slaves sang and answered each other as they moved off to their work stations.

If you get there before I do,"
Comin for to carry me home,
Tell all my friends I'm comin', too,
Comin' for to carry me home.

They continued singing as they began their work in the fields, the shops and pens, and their voices dropped to a low hum that went on throughout the day.

By now Joel and Eden had Journey cut down and covered with a clean sheet. The girl was on her feet but too weak to know which way to walk. Joel yelled over to Burdock,

"I want hot water and a clean bed!"

Esau signaled Glorybee, the housekeeper, who stood frozen in place nearby.

"Glorybee!!"

That's all he had to say, "Glorybee!" The woman jumped and started for the house.

"We got a room off the kitchen," she hollered as she ran off. "Won't need no stairs."

Joel took his medicine bag from the wagon. Journey leaned heavily on Eden as Joel's wife helped her to the house.

"You goin' to use that?" Esau asked Reuben, and indicated the lance.

"I'll wait," he answered and dragged the point down over Esau's chest to his belly. "I want you squealin' like a gut shot hog." Reuben cut him just enough and then joined Eden to help Journey. Blood seeped through the sheet and matted the cloth to her back.

"Reuben, Reuben," she said when she saw him.

"I'm here, child, I'm here," he answered.

"He hurt me so bad," she said and began to weep.

"He won't hurt you no more, child," spoke Reuben.

He loved this child so much he wished her pain was his.

Esau indicated the corpses of the dead slave catchers and ordered Prospero, who stood nearby, to:

"Get rid of 'em."

———— ∞∞∞ ————

Journey had been whipped hard. She lay face down on the bed as Joel worked over her. The lacerations were deep. They would heal, but the scars would be horrendous. Joel cleaned her wounds and covered them with salve. They would dry and close, but she would bear the evidence of her whipping until she died. Eden helped. When Joel finished, she covered the cuts with a clean cotton cloth. Reuben sat next to the bed and held Journey's hand. None of them could fathom the amount of pain she was in. She bore it well. The worst was over.

"Please don't let him brand me," she said to Reuben, her voice not much more than a whisper.

"No," he answered.

Esau appeared at the bedroom door.

"You'd've brought her to me when she was born this would never have happened," he said to Reuben. "You knew who she was. No Comanche give her to you."

"Her mother didn't want it."

"Well, damn it, of course she didn't want it! Don't mean you should've listened. You kept me from what was mine," said Esau.

"You taught me something today," Joel said.

"What's that?" asked Esau

"I never thought I could kill a man before," said Joel

"Welcome to the human race," Esau said, sounding strangely sad when he said it.

"If you're an example of what the human race has come to, I'd rather not be a part of it."

"How much?" asked Reuben.

"For what?" asked Esau.

"For Journey. How much you want?"

"You goin' to buy her?" Esau said it with derision.

"Shut up and listen to the man," yelled Eden suddenly, her wrath surprising them all.

"She'd fetch a good price," said Esau.

"Not with her back like that," countered Reuben.

Esau thought for a moment.

"Three thousand," he said.

"Like the cougar," said Reuben.

"Right," Esau said as he, too, realized the price of the two was the same. "Like the cougar."

"I bring you the lion, you give me the girl,"

"That your best offer?"

"It ain't no offer. It's a condition."

"The lion for her," repeated Esau.

"The lion for the girl. You brand her before I get back, and I swear you'll wear your own brand on your forehead before I'm through."

"You're an old man."

"You saw me out there."

"Still."

"The lion for the girl. Straight trade."

"Fine, old man. The lion for the girl. And I don't brand her 'til you come back without it, or somebody else gets it first. Watch your back, old man. I hear that lion's good at what he does."

From her bed, weak and in a whisper, "You can't go out there alone," said Journey.

"You rest. Let Joel and Eden care for you. Next time I see you, child, you'll be free." Reuben kissed her head, pushed past Esau, and walked from the room.

"Reuben!" Journey tried to call but he was gone. She struggled to get up.

"Stay still," said Eden.

"You can't let him do this." Journey could hardly speak, but fought to get up.

"You'd be no help. He'd have to look after you," argued Joel.

"Get me my buckskins." She struggled to sit, but couldn't and fell back.

"Drink this," he said. "It'll help," and poured an elixir into a glass for her to drink.

"This'll help?" she asked.

"Make you stronger," he said, knowing, as he held the glass to her lips, that it would put her to sleep.

"I'll find your buckskins," promised Eden.

"I need my Hawken, too."

"I'm sure Mr. Burdock will lend you one of his," said Eden.

The elixir was a strong dose of laudanum, and soon Journey was asleep.

———— ⧉ ————

She awakened into a cloud worse than sleep. The peace of opium carried no angry dreams, came without pain or fear, a gentle thermal that lifted and released her from the gravity of this world. However, in the half state to which she had come, the rawness returned, and lurking pain, a fretful knowledge that she was needed though she couldn't remember by whom or why. Journey rose up on one arm and saw a woman asleep in a rocking chair at the foot of her bed. Who was she? Who stole Journey's memory? She looked around and recognized nothing, felt fright and confusion until her eyes locked on a pile of buckskin clothing folded neatly on a bedside table. She realized the clothing was hers. She needed to reach it, put it on, go. Journey didn't know where or why she was going, only that she had to get there.

She sat up with both legs hanging over the side of the bed and reached for her buckskin leggings. She tried to pull them on, put her foot everywhere she could, but kept getting both legs caught in one leg or none at all, stood up on one and tried to put the other in, lost her balance, called for help. The woman at the foot of her bed jumped up and grabbed her to keep Journey from falling.

"Please, dear, get back in bed," she said. Her voice was kind. "Sit there. I'll help you. Drink this." So Journey drank and lay back, while the woman put a damp compress on her forehead, and soon the tender hush was hers once more.

Then it was daytime and Journey was sitting up in bed, while a woman held a bowl to her lips and fed her hot broth. It was Eden. Journey knew who it was. Her back was not so raw as it had been, and the broth was good. Suddenly, she knew who it was and what she had to do.

"Reuben," she said, "Where is Reuben?"

"He'll be back," said Eden.

"Reuben," she called.

"Here, child, drink this. Reuben will be back soon."

Eden held the glass for her so she could drink, and the next time she awoke it was nighttime. She knew by the silence that the ranch was asleep. Eden snored softly in the chair. Journey felt stronger than she had since the whipping.

"Be careful," she told herself, "Be careful."

She reached for her leggings, and this time had no trouble putting them on. Her moccasins were next, then the buckskin which hurt her back but not so much as before, so now it was time to stand and walk. Journey knew if Eden woke up she'd stop her and make her drink the elixir, which was a blessing but not now. Not now.

"Be careful," she told herself, "Be careful."

She stood and steadied herself against the bed, and when she was sure she took a step and held onto the bedside table, then two more steps and she was out the door. The wall would keep her from falling, though she didn't feel the need of it, not so much, but still.

"Be careful," she murmured to herself, "Be careful."

The night air was cool, came as a tonic, and brought her strength. Journey felt tall and able, but continued to brace herself wherever she could as she made her way from the house to the stable. The wind shifted, and she heard the young colt snort from his corral as he caught her scent. When he spotted her he ran over to the fence and stuck out his head for a scratch.

"Hey, boy, good to see you," she cooed, and let him nuzzle her. Journey's paint came over, too.

"Ready to ride, girl?," she asked. The paint danced in place and snickered happily. Prospero emerged from the stable to see what the ruckus was.

"Good to see you up," he said. "You sure took a beatin'."

"How long since?" she asked.

"Mus' be three days," answered the slave.

Journey was certain Reuben would be somewhere in Wild Horse Canyon by now. She'd need to stop at the cabin for her Hawken and some jerky, so she was anxious to get going.

"I could use a little help lifting my saddle. Would you mind gettin' it for me?" She'd be riding in tough terrain, rock strewn ups and downs, and knew it was better both for her and the horse to saddle up. He was about to say "yes" when he stopped mid thought.

"Can't do that, Journey," he stammered.

"Just lift it up for me," she said, "I'll do the rest."

"Mastuh Esau whup me for that," he replied.

"Go ahead, Prospero. Give her a hand," came Esau's voice from behind her. It startled her, even more so because he said nothing else, just stood there.

"I appreciate it," she said. "Better if there's two of us out there."

Esau simply rested his arms on the rail and watched while Prospero helped Journey saddle up. Before he opened the gate Prospero asked, "All right with you, Suh?" Esau nodded, and Journey rode out into the night with the colt alongside. She never thought to ask Esau why.

Pritta awoke when Journey rode up. Reuben had been in the mountains for two days. His dogs, Blue Dog, Loco, and Sadie, went with him. As Journey got her Hawken, balls, and powder, a buffalo hide to sleep on, plus flint and steel for a fire,

Pritta put together a sack of jerky, corn bread, and dried berries.

"Both come back," she said.

Journey kissed her goodbye and headed out, with the colt at a trot behind her.

She made the ridge at daybreak and followed it down into the canyon as the sun leapt free of the rock walls and brought color where there had only been bone and shadow. A recent rain, brisk but brief, muddied old tracks and made new ones stand out in sharp relief, making Journey's job easier. Reuben had made camp beside the creek where they'd camped before. The ashes were still warm, and there were dog tracks all around. He hadn't been gone long. Journey put down her buffalo hide next to his, let the horses water, and walked the tracks a few yards out of camp to try and determine his direction. She was relieved the tracks were so new. That meant he was most likely still safe. She knew she'd hear the dogs if he were onto anything. The colt caught a scent, lifted his head, and looked down canyon. A small band of horses was hurrying his way. He pranced in place. They were beautiful creatures, a strawberry roan, a bay, and a buttermilk cream with black ears. Journey figured them for fillies. They arrived maybe ten yards from the camp, and she could see that she was right.

"What do you think, boy," she said to the colt, "Are you looking for a girl? Are you looking for a dance?" He snorted happily. "Go on then," said Journey, slapped him on the rump, and sent him racing down canyon with the other horses.

"Be back in time for supper," she yelled after him, but Journey wasn't serious. Just a joke to make herself laugh. "You finished, girl?," she asked the paint, and gave the horse a berry as a treat. "Let's go, lady," she said, and led her by the reins as she studied the tracks. The only sound she heard were the footfalls of her horse.

Tracking is part sense and part sixth sense in equal portions. Some you see, some you suppose, some you learn, some you intuit. Reuben had taught Journey what he could see, but what he could not see he inferred, and much of this she had to learn for herself. Losing the trail did not mean it was the end of the trail. It only meant looking in a new way. It meant recognizing why the hair on your neck stands up or where a whiff of scent comes from, why your stomach becomes a knot or your eyes are drawn to what seems like empty space. It meant visualizing the animal when it wasn't there because it had been or would be; it meant internalizing the hunted. There had been times when Reuben was truly lost. At those times he stopped still, sat down, and breathed deeply, deliberately, slowly, slowly. He looked at the ground at his feet, looked up into the sky, and soon grew calm. He did not think in terms of the supernatural, so he offered no firm explanation why this worked, only that it did. What he wanted Journey to understand was that fear finds nothing.

The thing about a lion is that it places its hind leg in the same spot as its foreleg, so it leaves no back print at all, but this one, if it left any kind of track, would show a badly damaged right forepaw, thus making it easier to follow. Based on experience. Reuben knew he had to climb to get this animal, but the higher he went the rockier the terrain, and try tracking an animal over solid rock. So he relied on his dogs to pick up a scent. So far they hadn't. But the lion knew that he was there. Of that Reuben was sure, and on that point he was right. The lion stood atop a precipice with the sun behind him, making him nearly impossible to spot. Far below, no more than a speck in the vast wilderness, Reuben worked his way through the terrain. The dogs were out of sight, but they could be heard barking as they ran. Reuben rode across a rocky bench studded with juniper and pinon. He stopped and leaned down to study fresh spoor. Suddenly the pitch and timbre of the dogs' voices changed. Their barks became shrill and insistent, and when they did the lion's eyes narrowed and a rumble came from the depths of its throat.

The dogs were fighting their way up a steep, gravelly slope in wild lunges. Blue Dog's voice was high and sweet. As they charged up an incline that reached to the rim of the cliff, the lion turned and loped easily in the opposite direction. Reuben couldn't yet see the dogs but he knew they were climbing, and he picked his way after them between boulders big as cabins. Reuben was still a good way below, but now he spotted the dogs as they scrambled up the talus towards the rim, reached the top, and ran full out in the lion's direction, Blue Dog in the lead.

Reuben shifted direction, angling up the incline in a move designed to keep the dogs in his view, but slightly to his right as they ran the ridgeline. He wasn't looking where the lion might have been right then. He was looking ahead of the dogs to where the lion would be. Might be. It was a probable. At some point the lion would flash through an open space, and that's where the shot had to take him. Could take him. Maybe. You led the lion and shot through the open space an instant before the lion got there, and you played on the hope that shot and beast would collide. If the lion were to tree the shot would be stationary. Easier. Up ahead some yards was a stand of pine with crowns on thin upper trunks that rose just below the ridgeline.

The dogs were tonguing wildly now, which meant the lion was in their sight. Reuben thought it likely that the cat would leap from the ridge and tree in the first pine. It would think it was safe, and there Reuben would have his shot. But he saw the dogs pass above the pines, meaning the lion had passed by them as well. The big cat was running the dogs, making it hard for Reuben. It wasn't about to give itself up. It had lived a long time and collected a gut full of tricks, and it knew the territory in such a way that a man could only wonder. The ridge angled suddenly upward, and as it did the lion appeared and jumped over to a ledge, making it impossible for the dogs to reach him. They stood above him, berserk and baying wildly. The lion leapt to another ledge and another, and then launched itself into space, dropping down into the crown of the first tree. Was it possible? No, it was not possible, only there it was. Reuben had his shot. The crown of the tree bent in an arc towards the ground from the lion's weight. Reuben thought the cat would drop, but it didn't. It hung on as the trunk snapped back up again and catapulted the lion into the crown of the next tree, and then it catapulted into a second tree and a third, a fourth, and then a final twenty foot leap from the crown of that last tree to the rim of the cliff on the other side. There it disappeared. Vanished. Gone. Reuben could barely grasp what he had just seen. The dogs ceased their barking and stared out over the trees as if they, too, were amazed.

———— ∞∞∞ ————

The day's hunt had taken Reuben well into the afternoon. There was no point in going further that day. The dogs were worn out, his horse was tired, and so was he. He should head back to camp and get a fresh start in the morning.

Journey had decided to turn back long before. She'd heard the dogs for only a short while, but lost them when they slipped further into the distance. She knew Reuben would return to camp before nightfall, and so decided to get it ready for him. He would not expect to see her there, and would not expect fresh fish cooking on a spit. She'd surprise him on both counts. Journey hobbled her paint and let the horse graze while she sharpened a stick into a spear and headed up stream to a pool she'd seen. When Reuben returned, she had the coffee on and two fat trout cooking on a spit. The colt and three fillies had come back as well, and nuzzled Journey as they searched for more dried berries, so deliciously sweet. Pritta had given her plenty, so Journey nibbled at them, too. On his way down the mountain Reuben saw the fire and smelled the cooking fish. He thought it might be Journey and was delighted to see he was right. She told him Esau had let her go. Neither of them understood why, but there was hot coffee, biscuits, and plenty more to eat, and they wished for no company other than what they had. After dinner they sat back against the rocks while Reuben smoked his pipe and told her a story.

He was living in Comanche territory at the time, so long ago. Some white settlers had moved into a nook of it. The land they built on was mostly desolate, so the Comanche hadn't bothered them, yet. Pretty soon they put up a church and called it the Lord's Valley Assembly of God. It stood in a pretty little clearing in some woods reachable by a dirt path. A cougar caught onto them quick and began preying on their stock. The preacher figured more prayers were what was needed, but everybody was afraid to walk through the woods to their little church. The preacher boasted he'd walk through the woods and back, and he'd do it at night. "I love God and put my trust in Him," he said, "I'll be safe." The members of his congregation stood at the edge of the woods and begged him not to do it, but the man wouldn't listen. "God's goin' to protect me," he told them, and he believed it, too. So, he walked through the woods without incident, got a Bible from the church to prove he'd been there, and started back. Midway, the lion jumped him, bit him, shredded his clothes, and nearly killed him. The preacher finally managed to send that murderous fiend to hell with his Bowie knife stuck deep in its innards and made his way out of the woods. Man was in mortal pain. He passed out from his wounds and didn't wake up for three and a half days, which time nobody knew whether he'd live or die. On the morning of the fourth day he finally came out of it. "What happened back in the woods?" Everybody'd been dying to ask him. "Well, brothers and sisters," the preacher said, "God is good. I love Him, and I put my faith in Him. He'll help you through a lot of things, but, brothers and sisters, good as God is, He ain't worth a damn in a cat fight."

Their campfire was only a twinkle in the wilderness. They knew the lion was out there, but it wouldn't come near the fire. Most likely, they figured, he was up high but certainly aware of them. They were right that he was aware of them, but wrong about where he was.

Their bellies were full, and they'd counted stars. Now Reuben and Journey slept soundly. Both knew her freedom depended on the success of the hunt, but they would stay out as long as it took, and they had their freedom now, didn't they? Her back remained raw in places, and there was no doubt she'd bear the scars for the rest of her life, but she meant to bear them proudly as a soldier bears his wounds, signs of the fight, signs she never gave in.

A rabbit crept just inside the circle of light thrown by the fire. Sadie, the youngest dog, woke up and smelled it. She whined, tried to control herself, but the temptation was too great and she began to slink forward on her belly. A young pup. What did you expect? A rabbit. A fat morsel. Pungent and mouthwatering. Sadie wanted that rabbit. It blotted out every other instinct she possessed, and she intended to have it. She was a few feet away from Reuben when he reached out to touch her and found she wasn't there. He opened his eyes and saw her slinking away.

"Get back here, Sadie," he ordered. "I said get back here, girl!" Sadie whined out a complaint—"I said get back here!"— tucked her tail reluctantly, and crawled back where Reuben slapped her good. "You stay still, understand?" Sadie lay down with a whine and a groan, but she put her head on her fore-paws and was soon again asleep. The next morning Reuben went out and looked for sign. He found it. The tall grass outside the light thrown by the fire was matted down, still warm with a musky odor. The lion had been there all night and had only just slipped away.

Esau had been awake all night as well. He sat before the fire in his library and tried to read, but the port blurred his vision and when that was gone the brandy didn't help, instead sending him deeper and deeper into his own slime. His mother died a vile and disgusting bag of rags. To see her was to glimpse a denizen of the valley of the lepers. To touch her was even worse, and yet she counted on that very image to earn her daily bread.

"Please, sir," she'd croak, "Please, sir," and proffer her bony fingers for half a penny. Esau didn't know where she'd been buried or if she'd been buried at all. A sawbones might have taken what remained for a dissection. Esau didn't care. He'd come far from those days and rarely thought of them. So why had she crept up on him now? For a gold piece? He had them in his pocket, more than he ever dreamed of when he pounded mugs on the streets of London. *Here! Take what you want. Just go away! Let me think of better things! Let me think of fine cigars, a box of teak, a musket engraved in gold and measured to the length of my arms, suckling pig when I want on a porcelain platter.*

What didn't he have? He had it all and no need to dwell on the time he didn't. Esau was the lord of all he surveyed. He had dominion over man and beast. His fields were fertile and his gardens lush. Other men sought his advice. He'd taken people from the darkness and provided them with clothes and shelter for all their days, clothes and shelter and food they grew with their own hands on their own plots. Livy could have been a lady here, could have had a life of ease with a whole household at her beck and call. There could have been no marriage, of course, but still, a place of respect. Keeper of the lord's house. His right hand and his left. She could have lived to see her granddaughter grow to loveliness. Instead, she chose to hang him. Lilly Rose chose to run away. Journey chose the whip. That was a mistake. He could have sold her for a fortune. Should have put her in his pocket quick. But now she was damaged goods and wouldn't fetch half that, and, anyway, he did not want to sell her, did not want her gone. Down deep he did not.

So it would have to be his shot that killed the lion. She would see that he was a man the equal of Reuben. No, the better. After all, whose daughter was she? Not Reuben's, but his.

What had Reuben done with his life? Instead of horses the half-breed had three mangy dogs. Curs. What was he, anyway? Apache? Mexican? He had no hacienda, and his woman had no nose. Esau hunted with a rifle custom made. He'd driven nails with it. The lion marauded his ranch and his property. His! Esau didn't need another man to do his killing for him.

The ash from his cigar had fallen off and burned a hole in the upholstery. He smacked it hard to make sure it was out. "Prospero!" he called, and promptly tripped over the ottoman. "Prospero, saddle my horse!"

"Esau," he muttered to himself, "The boy can't hear you from here." Then "Glorybee, wake up!" He called for his housekeeper. "Wake up, goddamnit. I need bread, bacon, canteen. Wake up!"

He stumbled to the kitchen where she slept and tore the cover off her bed. "Goddamnit, girl, I need powder, balls, food, wine!" Glorybee, half awake, still in her nightclothes, jumped up and paid heed. "Prospero!" Esau yelled out the kitchen door, "Prospero, goddamn you, boy! Wake the hell up! I need my horse! I need oats! My saddle scabbard. Rope. Come on, boy! Turn loose the goddamn bloodhound! Glory, get me something the girl had on!"

"I've said it once; I've said it twice, and, trust me, I'll say it ten times more: That cat didn't get to be old by being stupid," said Reuben, who stood there in wonderment at the canniness of the creature. "Sometimes I even wonder if he ain't aware of every move we make, and this chase is just a game to him."

Journey stood there with Reuben at the spot where the lion spent the night, not fifty feet away, the canyon wind in his face catching the scent of everyone and everything at the campsite while cloaking his. It even occurred to Reuben that the cat had actually used the rabbit to bait the dogs, let the rabbit live so the dogs would chase it, just like Sadie would've if Reuben hadn't called her back.

"You figure a lion actually thinks like that?" asked Journey

"Not in so many words. Not in words at all. They're born with a lot and then experience learns them the rest. They store up stuff and it comes out when they need it," said Reuben. "This one saw the rabbit and waited for the dog. That tells me somethin'."

Right then all three dogs were snorting and snuffling over the lion's fresh scent, a smell so pungent they seemed to swallow it whole, jumping around Reuben like puppies, begging and whining to be cut loose: *Lemme go lemme go lemme go!*

"Where to?" asked Journey

"That's the good part. We won't know 'til we get there," answered Reuben. "Go on," he ordered the dogs, "Go find it!" The dogs shot out of camp like they were launched from a catapult. The colt, after a handful of berries, had long since taken his fillies up canyon. Reuben and Journey mounted up and followed behind the dogs at an easy pace. This was hardscrabble territory. You didn't want your horse to break a leg.

Esau's brain was a blur. Prospero told him he had no call being on a horse in that condition, and was snapped at—"Mind your own damn business!"—for his advice. The stable hand would have been whipped for his thoughts just then. *Fall off and bust your mean and ugly head wide open,* went through his mind. *Bleed to death in a ditch with all your sins,* was another. Of course, Prospero didn't say any such a thing, simply handed the master his horsewhip and prayed for the worst. Glorybee handed Esau the food, wine, and one of Journey's underthings. The man mounted his blood bay battle stallion, perfect for a charge in full armor, but thoroughly insane for a mountain pony. Glorybee and Prospero shared a look, each knowing what the other was thinking: *Good Lord, take this man and send him to the dust bin.* Esau plunged his heels into the horse's ribs and set off swaying sideways in the saddle, with visions of glory in his head.

———— ∞∞∞ ————

Reuben and Journey picked their way cautiously through a blow down that appeared to be a giant child's set of pick-up sticks. It had once been a large stand of pine, but years of pummeling by blustery weather had laid it low. The dogs, of course, bounded over tree after tree, barely slowing down. The lion had been through here. Once the two riders got into it, Reuben wished they had gone around it and thought of something he learned along ago. If you can step on it, step over it; if you can step over it, step around it. That way you'll live to climb more mountains. Don't forget again, old man. You've climbed a lot of mountains and plan to climb some more. Don't forget. The lion didn't. He set you up, and you fell into it.

It was noon when they cleared the blow down, stopped for lunch at the mouth of a small side canyon, and rested the horses. This would be a terrible place to be in a rainstorm. A flash flood would sweep you away along with everything else, grind you up and spit you out—but there would be no rain today, and it was a pleasant place to lean back and rest. The dogs were out there someplace, but they were quiet and unless you could hear them there was nothing to do but sit and relax awhile, gnaw some jerky, talk or not, enjoy each other's company. How many days in a lifetime can you stop and do just that?

———— ∞∞ ————

Esau Burdock was behind them, though neither party knew the other was there. He'd arrived at the campsite in Wild Horse Canyon with a raging headache. Jouncing around on horseback hadn't helped much. He was a couple of hours behind them, but right then he was more interested in losing his headache than finding those two. His dog, once the hound got a whiff of the scent of Journey's buffalo hide, became delirious. He took off and wouldn't be called back, so Esau had no choice but to follow him. Esau could either sit still and have a headache or take off after the dog and have a headache. At this juncture, he was a most unhappy individual who swallowed another mouthful of wine and went for the dog.

———— ∞∞ ————

His paw hurt him, the right front, the one he'd torn free from the trap. At times like this, when it ached, he went to a hot spring deep in the mountains and soaked it. In all the years he'd been using the spring, he never detected a human scent there, and so he felt safe, unhurried. About a mile before the spring, there stood an "archipelago" of boulders, enormous rocks each separated by a distance of about twenty feet. There were fifteen of them, set down in a row as if by the same giant child's hand that set the blow down of pine trees. Without a single footfall on the ground, he'd leapt from boulder to boulder and lost the dogs. Tracks all around the spring showed that it was used by many animals including an aging grizzly bear, but even the griz knew better than to visit when the lion was around. Two cranky old animals in the same place would have meant pitched battle. Neither one would have deliberately ventured into the other's territory knowing the other was there. The one thing that kept the lion from perfect peace was the mad chattering of the squirrels in the trees, warning the rest of the creatures that the lion was there.

As for humans he'd seen them close and seen them far, although he'd never confronted one head on until that two-legged creature that drove him off the horse. The closest he'd come was when he took small children, plus the one time he was caught in the trap. He was younger then, lured in by the trumpeting of a wounded elk, unaware that it was a hunter doing the calling. He'd come in slow, stealthy, as was the way with cougars, lying still in the underbrush until his instincts told him he could move, but he was a young cat who still had trouble downing large prey by himself. It had been a dreary winter, and this time his hunger bested him. The trap was well hidden by brush and stones, and baited with a chunk of fresh elk meat, and the cat stepped right into it. The panther was stunned, caterwauled, and tried to pull away, but he was caught, and almost immediately a shot plowed a furrow in the thick skin on the back of his neck. The shot was high. He spotted the shooter at fifty yards, reloading for a second. The hunter, assuming the painter wasn't going anywhere, moved closer, and the cat, in his desperation, tore free, leaving part of his paw stuck in the trap. Had the hunter's first shot been true, or had the cat stepped cleanly into the trap, the living, breathing beast would have been no more. With all the prey he'd taken the rest of his life, the cat had never been bested again.

Now he continued to lie there with his paw soaking in the water, shutting out the squirrels and ignoring a young deer that meandered along. When the deer caught the cougar's scent nearby, its heart jumped like it had been pounded by a ram, and an instant later it disappeared into a thicket and kept on going. The lion paid it no mind at all. But it wasn't long before something did yank his attention and hung onto it: the urgent yelp of a hound dog, a different voice from the three he had lost. Sound carried in the thin mountain air. The dog was a good way off, but still the lion's instinct told him not to ignore it.

Reuben and Journey heard the yelping, too. They were on the move again, but their dogs hadn't picked up anything new. They were just running at random, quartering back and forth, onto nothing, though they perked up once they heard the new one.

"Who the hell is that?" asked Reuben, but Journey didn't know either. "Blue Dog, Loco, Sadie, get goin!," ordered Reuben, giving the three of them permission to take off after the fourth. For a long time, the new dog's voice was the only one they heard, but that changed when the four dogs finally connected. Blue Dog was barking treed, and then he wasn't. The dogs were definitely onto the lion, though he was still ahead of them and on the move. Reuben and Journey wished they could be with them, but the two were on talus and had to lead their horses.

Four distinct dogs could be heard, only now they were coming closer. The lion must have switched direction. Reuben knew the territory well, but the lion knew it better.

"Painter's got somethin' in mind," he told Journey. They quartered to the west instead of north dead on. By now it was mid-afternoon. The sun was lower in the sky, so its horizontal rays created more shadow. It might be harder to see the lion than if the sun were directly overhead, but the trail was hot, and they would have to take the shot that presented itself.

They crossed the talus slope to the other side, remounted, and rode down a sandy ridge. At the bottom of the ridge they reached a plateau that cut west and eventually dropped off steeply on both sides, creating a funnel effect that channeled the riders forward. The dogs were certainly closer now, all four of them voicing wildly. About a mile ahead the riders could see a steep, nearly vertical rock wall that soared over the area by a good one thousand feet. From the sound of the dogs, that's where they were headed, too. The surface of the funnel was hard and smooth, so the riders touched their horses into a fast trot and closed in on the cliff. The flat plain over which they rode dropped off on each side to a deadly precipice. There was not much room to maneuver. The riders had little margin for error. The dogs appeared ahead and reached the base of the cliff, where they fell all over each other trying to get purchase and climb. Neither Reuben nor Journey could see the cat, but they knew he was there and closed in as quickly as they could. All of a sudden, when they were still fifty yards away, a large blood bay stallion burst out of a side canyon with Esau Burdock, still swaying sideways but hanging on. He saw Reuben and Journey as well, pulled his rifle from its scabbard, and kicked his horse forward as fast as it would go.

Now the lion was visible, too, perched on a shelf maybe fifteen feet up the face of the cliff, raging furiously at the dogs below. Reuben didn't know how she did it, but Sadie, the youngest, was actually inching her way up and nearly just below the lion when the cat swatted her on the head and sent her practically decapitated to the ground. That's when Esau took his shot. It went wild. Reuben and Journey heard it ricochet off the rocks. Esau's mount panicked. It had never been fired off before and rocketed forward, out of control, towards the cliff where it couldn't stop, reared on its hind legs, and blindly tried to scramble over the rocks up the face. Reuben

and Journey were there by then. Each jumped out of the saddle with their rifles ready, but the big cat launched itself off the
shelf and onto Esau, driving him from the saddle to the
ground. The man managed to get one hand down the lion's
throat, tried to hold the cat off with the other, but the lion bit
and tore, even though Burdock fought him mightily. Neither
Reuben nor Journey had a shot. The lion and the man rolled
over and over, locked in a blood duel, but the man was no
match for the lion. The lion was underneath, ripping apart
Esau's midsection, but when the lion rolled topside again
Reuben knew he'd better shoot or Esau surely was going to
die. His shot smashed the beast in the hips, but didn't stop it
and only enraged the cat more. Journey stopped thinking. If
she had been thinking she probably wouldn't have done what
she did, but the girl was on instinct and jumped on the lion's
back with her legs clamped around its midsection and her
arms clamped around its throat. The pair toppled backwards.

The lion left Esau alone and turned on Journey. Its hind
legs were useless, splayed out straight behind it, but its massive
shoulders and forepaws propelled it forward onto the girl.
Reuben had no time to reload and fire again. He heard himself
scream for the lion to stop, as if that would do any good, but
suddenly the frantic whinny of a wild horse lacerated the air as
the chestnut colt appeared from the side canyon and bore
down upon the lion. It stomped the beast, kicked it in the head,
and gave Journey the space to crawl out from under. The big
cat turned on the colt, and now the two animals faced each
other. That the cat could not use his hind legs seemed to make
no difference to him. As the colt reared to stomp him the lion
flipped over and raked the colt's belly. The horse backed off a
step, then came down hard on the lion's chest. Journey heard
the crunch of bones. The cat was sorely hurt, righted itself and
tried to crawl away. It was then that the horse spun around

and caught the lion with such a devastating kick that the cat went staggering towards the edge of the precipice. The colt spun and connected again, and this time the cat went flying out over the edge where it clawed the air, spit, and shrieked horribly as it fell to its death on the rocks hundreds of feet below. At that the colt spun around again, went to Journey, and nuzzled the girl, caring for her in its way as the girl had cared for it.

The two men were speechless. Drunk as he was, the moment was not lost on Esau. Journey had come through with only minor scratches, hugged the colt around his neck, and nuzzled him back. He whinnied happily and danced in place. Esau was hurt and bleeding badly, but not so much that he couldn't stagger to his feet and go to Journey. The colt snorted nervously as Esau approached, but Journey simply said, "Good boy. Good boy," and the young horse calmed down. Esau was still speechless. He couldn't think of what to say or where to start. Reuben came over, stroked the young horse, thanked him, and hugged the child who was so very precious to him.

"You're free, child," Esau said to Journey, "And the horse is yours." Then he sat down on the ground because he no longer had the strength to stand. It was then that the three fillies—the bay, the roan, and the buttermilk—appeared at the mouth of the side canyon. In their way they called for the colt. He nuzzled Journey, then looked at her as if waiting for the girl to tell him what to do.

"You're free, boy," she said, "You're free," and slapped him gently on the rump. "Go on now," she said and sent him away.

Acknowledgments

As for getting a novel published, it takes a village. For starters, Jules Older and I go back to 1954 when, as high school freshman, we were the only Jewish boys to flunk out of the "A" course. That's been our bond ever since, so, when Joe Healy, a writer/editor friend of Jules from Vermont asked him to recommend a writer for an anthology Joe was editing called, *When Bears Attack: Close Encounters of the Terrifying Kind*, Jules recommended me. Joe published my true life story and was generous enough to read an early draft of Journey. It was Joe who sent it to Skyhorse, and Steve Price who shepherded it to acceptance by Jay Cassell. I'm grateful to Skyhorse for their faith in my book, for the gentle editing that maintained its colloquial tone, and for the push that drove me to make it even more creative than it was before.

Without a doubt, the day Morgan State College (now University), in Baltimore, Maryland, an historically black school, allowed me to attend was the most fortunate day of my life. I'd failed out of too many other schools to count, and had recently been honorably discharged from the Marines with few life skills other than the ability to construct a pontoon bridge in a jungle under fire. June, 1962. Morgan accepted me provisionally and then full-time. I was the only white guy in the student body, and the civil rights movement was coming into its own. The times were electric. My first play was written and produced there, and then taken to New York. A brilliant faculty. An embracing student body. Morgan changed my life forever.

In the years before *Journey* ever came to the attention of Skyhorse, there were readers, of this manuscript and many others, whose encouragement has been invaluable. Eric Rickstad, Reuben Hermanson Sack, Casey Szcieska, Dyanne Asimow, David Evans, Peter Harris and Carrie Shea read various versions of *Journey*, buoyed my spirit and kept me in the fight. Other friends and readers who have been there for me as I wrote and wrote and kept on writing: David Freeman, Brooke Adams, Lynne Adams, Joel Foreman, Ellen Foreman Sack, Jon Foreman, David Fallon, Gary Lennon, Jerome Gary, Judith Bernstein, Carrie Robbins, Judith Ren-Lay, Ellen and Peter Stern, Lynne Schwabe, Debra and Billy McGuire, Chan Chandler, Alex and Eleanor Schub, Jon Taplin, Roger Hendricks Simon, Stephen Simon, Scott Tschirgi, Lenny B and Kathy, Steve Adams, and Lexi Beach.

And for so many days and nights, months and years, myriad moments of joy and happiness, there has been my family, my wife and partner, Jamie Donnelly, and my two children, Sevi D and Madden Rose, my gem stones, my gifts, my blessings. Without them there would be no words at all.